Praise for *New Finnish Grammar*

"The story of a mysteriously wounded man sent to Helsinki amid
the chaos of the second world war to try to rebuild his memory
and identity, it's a strange, tender portrait of Finnish legends and
language-learning, loneliness and human connection."
Justine Jordan Fiction Highlights of 2011 in *The Guardian*

"The title is odd, the cover is grey and the author is a besuited
Eurocrat. But beneath these unflamboyant exteriors lie a colourful
story. It has taken 10 years, the dedication of a small UK publisher
and a perfect-pitch translation to deliver Diego Marani's first
novel in English. When it came out in Italian, reviewers called it a
masterpiece and it won several prizes. Since then Marani has written
five more novels and become a Euro-celebrity."
Rosie Goldsmith in *The Independent*

"...a subtle exploration of how language shapes our sense of
ourselves..."   Adrian Turpin in *The Financial Times*

"...we soon forget we are reading an English translation of an Italian
novel. Sheer narrative vim is one reason for this... What gives *New
Finnish Grammar* its true interest, however, is its evocation of a place
and language foreign to the author yet, to all appearances, intimately
familiar."   Oliver Ready in *The Times Literary Supplement*

"One somehow knows that this couldn't have been written by an
English writer. It has a thoroughly European sensibility: intellectual,
melancholy, mysterious, imbued with a sense of tragedy and history."
Brandon Robshaw in *The Independent on Sunday*

"Diego Marani ist the parfait persona to tell this story. In his novel, a man wakes up with no memory and is forced to relearn language. And the poor bloke happens to end up in Finland. Finnish grammar is notoriously intricate, counting 15 cases for nouns — including one for nouns which are absent. It's an abessive case of amnesia."

Fleur Macdonald in *The Spectator*

"...a thoughtful, idiosyncratic book and, in its utter disdain for the conventions of literary realism, entirely to be applauded."

Joanna Kavenna in *The Literary Review*

"There is an unyieldingness at the heart of Diego Marani's novel. He presents a world where heroism is expended in a futile task, friendship is sacrificed to despair, and help is rendered in such a way as to further the disaster. Yet this book is full of riches: a landscape so solidly created one can hear the ice crack, a moving examination of what makes a human being, and a restless brooding over the ideas of memory, belonging and identity (all three main characters are in some way lost). It is written in mirror-smooth prose and superbly translated. The story, finally, can't fail."

Anita Mason in *The Warwick Review*

"As well as raising questions concerning psyche, identity and nationality, Sampo's confused agony is quite simply one of the most incisive reflections of the trauma that befell Europe during that period that one might ever read."   Oliver Basciano in *ArtReview*

"...the book is beautifully written, poetic and mysterious. It has much philosophical wisdom that will be long remembered after one has read the book."   Rose Lapira in *Malta Today*

"I know that it is a book that I will be thrusting into peoples hands for years to come urging them to buy it, read it and spread the word. It is the least that I can do for the pleasure that it has given me."

Broad Conversation from Blackwell's Bookshop in Oxford

Diego Marani

New
Finnish
Grammar

Translated by Judith Landry

Dedalus

This book has been published with the support of Ministero Affari Esteri Italiano and
Arts Council England, London.

Published in the UK by Dedalus Limited,
24-26, St Judith's Lane, Sawtry, Cambs, PE28 5XE
email: info@dedalusbooks.com
www.dedalusbooks.com

ISBN 978 1 903517 94 9

Dedalus is distributed in the USA by SCB Distributors,
15608 South New Century Drive, Gardena, CA 90248
email: info@scbdistributors.com   web: www.scbdistributors.com

Dedalus is distributed in Australia by Peribo Pty Ltd.
58, Beaumont Road, Mount Kuring-gai, N.S.W. 2080
email: info@peribo.com.au

Publishing History
First published in Italy in 2000
First published by Dedalus in May 2011
Reprinted in June, July, September, October 2011 and January 2012

Nuova Grammatica Finlandese © copyright RCS Libri S.p.A.- Milano Bompiani 2000
Translation copyright © Judith Landry 2011

The Author

Diego Marani was born in Ferrara in 1959. He works as a senior linguist for the European Union in Brussels.

Every week he writes a column for a Swiss newspaper about current affairs in Europanto, a language that he has invented.

His collection of short stories in Europanto, *Las Adventures des Inspector Cabillot*, will be published by Dedalus in May 2012 at the same time as his second novel, *The Last of the Vostyachs*.

His most recent novel *Il Cane did Dio* will be published in Italy in 2012 and by Dedalus in 2013.

The Translator

Judith Landry was educated at Somerville College, Oxford where she obtained a first class honours degree in French and Italian. She combines a career as a translator of works of fiction, art and architecture with part-time teaching.

Her translations for Dedalus are: *New Finnish Grammar* by Diego Marani, *The House by the Medlar Tree* by Giovanni Verga, *The Devil in Love* by Jacques Cazotte, *Prague Noir:The Weeping Woman on the Streets of Prague* by Sylvie Germain and *Smarra & Trilby* by Charles Nodier.

To Simona, Alessandro and Elisabetta

Ei Suomi ole mikään kieli, se on tapa istua penkin päässä karvat korvilla.

Paavo Haavikko

Prologue

My name is Petri Friari, I live at no. 16 Kaiser-Wilhelmstrasse, Hamburg and I work as a neurologist at the city's university hospital.

I found this manuscript on 24 January 1946 in a trunk in the military hospital in Helsinki, together with a sailor's jacket, a handkerchief with the letters S.K. embroidered on it, three letters, a volume of the Kalevala *and an empty bottle of* koskenkorva. *It is written in a spare, indeed broken and often ungrammatical Finnish, in a school notebook where pages of prose alternate with lists of verbs, exercises in Finnish grammar and bits cut out from the Helsinki telephone directory. Some pages are illegible, others contain just sequences of words without any apparent logic, drawings, foreign names, and headlines taken from the* Helsingin Sanomat. *Often the narrative proceeds by way of scraps cut out from newspapers, repeated each time a similar situation occurs, and fleshed out by others, in a wide variety of linguistic registers. My knowledge of the facts which lay behind this document has enabled me to reconstruct the story that it tells, to rewrite it in more orthodox language and to fill in some of the gaps. I myself have often had to intervene, adding linking passages of my own to tie up unrelated episodes. Adjectives left in the margins, nouns doggedly declined in the more complex cases of the Finnish language, all traced the outlines of a story which was well-known to me. In this way I have been able to coax these pages to yield up something that they were struggling in vain to tell. Using the scalpel of memory, I carved out words which ached like wounds I had believed to be long healed.*

Since I bore witness to many of the events and conversations recorded here, I have been able to piece them accurately together. In this I was greatly helped by Miss Ilma Koivisto, a nurse in the military medical corps who, like myself, was personally acquainted with the author of these pages.

The reader should not take this document as a reliable account of historical events, nor expect it to obey the laws of scientific observation. All it does is to tell one incredible human story. Twenty-eight years after having fled Helsinki, I had gone back, my sole reason being to track down the man who, as a result of a cruel misunderstanding on my part, had been unintentionally driven towards a fate which was not his own. But all that remains of him is this exercise book. Plagued with remorse, I set myself to unpicking the jumbled skein of this manuscript, feeling that the least I could do was to honour its writer by ensuring that he was remembered, and also perhaps to reconstruct my own story, my own identity, through other eyes. But it was many years before I could bring myself to offer these pages to the public (together with the annotations I added at the time), before they vanished, and me with them, once and for all. If there is no denying that it was my error which led the author of this manuscript to his tragic end, may I not at least plead the exceptional nature of the times as some excuse? The extreme uncertainty of those wartime days, when I was surrounded by death and suffering, caused muddled emotion to prevail over lucid reason, despite the fact that reason has so often served me well. At times, fate makes us the instrument of its designs, dragoons us into becoming unwitting accomplices in its savagery. Like this man, I too am an exile. But while he felt affection and gratitude for Finland, I have unfinished business with this country. Throughout all these years, I have tried to suppress my hatred for whoever it was who killed my father. Resisting the siren call of revenge, I have always sought to cherish the memory of the country which, after all, is still my own; I have kept up and cultivated my language, making each word a prayer with which I hoped to seek forgiveness for my father and, for myself, the promise of return.

And all to no avail. Time has sent shards of rancour through the clefts of my being, and it is these foreign bodies which shape my feelings: they take on monstrous form the moment they are born. Everything within me bears their mark, and redemption is no longer possible. My country continues to reject me, to fend me off, accusing me of yet another crime: that of having set the author of these pages on a mistaken course, thus wreaking his destruction.

Upstanding men, men of integrity, may serve as witnesses that what I did I did in all good faith. If Doctor Friedrich Reiner had found the handkerchief with the initials S.K. even a day earlier, the fate of Massimiliano Brodar would have been different, as would my own. One fine June day, when the smell of the sea is borne along the city streets, making every white building a sailing ship, I might have gone back to Helsinki, ready to forgive in order to be forgiven. But perhaps a hostile God had already settled everything, and Massimiliano Brodar is merely an instrument of my damnation.

Return to Helsinki

Doctor Friari's eyes were the first living thing I saw emerging out of nothingness. Preceded by a rustle of starched cotton, he appeared before me, haloed in blue, and stayed there for a time, watching me carefully. But the shifting blur of my disturbed vision prevented me from making out the outlines of his face. It was as though everything were bathed in a dense liquid, which slowed down movement and deadened sound. What followed were days when nothing seemed to move, whose surface was barely rippled by muffled voices, shadows behind glass, long silences somehow tinged with yellow. I tried to keep my eyes open for as long as possible, to blink away the misty blur so as to see the doctor looking at me. But even the briefest effort was promptly rewarded by a sharp stab which caused me to close my eyes again. I could feel the pain welling up from behind my temples, buzzing and swelling like a swarm of bees before settling behind my eyes. Sometimes a sudden wave of warmth would sweep over me; then I would sweat and feel my head throbbing beneath the bandages. The nurses must have noticed, because suddenly a glass bubble with a drip would appear beside me, and something cold would be applied to my arm. Then gradually the stabbing pains became less frequent, and things around me began to take on greater solidity. The blue halo became a porthole, the long silences were now less tinged with yellow, and the darkness was lit up by a night-light, screwed into a niche in the wall of the corridor.

So, I was on a ship. I could feel its slight pitching, though I could detect no sense of movement. I was aware that all was not well with me, but I saw and felt in a detached way, as though only a part of me were alive and sentient, and floating in something that was alien to me. As I recalled much later, in those days of gradual reawakening my brain was indifferent to my bodily state, as though it no longer had either the will or strength to bother with it. Now, before the doctor's visits, two nurses would come to seat me in an armchair by the porthole. I had noted that they were Red Cross Nurses, and even in my confusion I remembered that there was a war on. I also thought that I might be a survivor of some wartime operation. But I could not remember who I was, nor did I have the curiosity to do so. My thoughts seemed to well up out of nothingness and then sink down again into the porous soil of my unfocused consciousness. Later on, I thought back to that sensation almost with regret. For just a few, marvellous days I was untouched by memory, free from recall, released from pain. I was just a bundle of cells, a primitive organism like those which peopled the earth millions of years ago. From my chair I could see the other side of the cabin, my camp bed, the bedside table. And above all, even if it was an effort to turn my head, I could see the sea beyond the porthole. Making it to the chair must have been a great step forward, because now Doctor Friari would smile when he came to visit me. He would shine a light into my eyes and examine them, easing them open with his fingers. He would bring down the little folding table fixed to the wall, lay out coloured cardboard shapes on it and ask me to say what they reminded me of. He always seemed very pleased with my reactions, and would jot things down in a notebook.

At first, our meetings took place in silence, taking the form of a dance of movements, courteous gestures and affable nods. After a few days, Doctor Friari began to talk to me, but using words that were different from those he addressed to the nurses – ones with rounder, more full-bodied, lingering sounds. I was as yet unaware of the tragedy that had befallen me, I did not know that the trauma of which I was the victim had debarred me from the world of language. My mind was a ship whose moorings had been shattered by a storm. I could see the landing stage bobbing not far off, and I thought that as I regained my strength I would be able to reach it. What I did not know was that the wind of desperation would carry me ever further out to sea. I could not understand the words that Doctor Friari spoke, nor did I feel any instinct or desire to answer him. But this did not worry me. Without really thinking, I put all this down to the wound I had sustained, to the immense tiredness from which I was gradually recovering. Furthermore, though only in the vaguest possible way, the hazy notion of a foreign language was surfacing in my mind, and this, as far as I could see, would explain why I failed to understand the doctor's words.

As I learned later, right from those early days, the doctor was speaking to me in Finnish, his own language, which he believed also to be my own. He hoped that the soft, welcoming words of my mother tongue would soothe my pain and lessen my bewilderment, making me feel that I was among friends. I did not try to talk because I simply did not feel the need. All linguistic feeling, all interest in words, had died away. I could not speak any language, I no longer knew which was my own. But I was unaware of this: a subtle veil, like a form of hypnosis, was shielding me from the violent colours of reality.

One morning Doctor Friari opened up a map of Europe on the table and gestured to me to do something I could not understand. I thought that this was some new exercise and set myself to observing the green and brown patches, the jagged indentations of the blue sea, the deep furrows of the rivers. I knew that this was a map, the shapes of the countries meant something to me, I had already seen them on countless

15

occasions. I had a clear idea of the things that I was seeing, but my understanding seemed trapped just below the outer skin of reality. I recognized those outlines just as I did every other object around me, but I could not put a name to them. My mind jibbed at any effort in that direction; as I noted later, it was as though it no longer had the tools to do so. My body, my hands had begun to move again. The movement of my joints gave me the sensation of having a body. I would lay hands on everything I saw: by touching things I would regain some knowledge of them. But my mind no longer knew how to link words and things; detached from me yet alive within me, it moved around without my being able to catch up with it, like a fish in a tank apparently expanded by the water and the glass, so that the edges too seem far away even when they are near. So I no longer knew what I was supposed to do with that map.

By way of encouragement, the doctor pointed a finger at a stumpy green strip fretworked with blue. I looked first at his eyes and then at the map, frowning in a state of growing confusion. Then at last I understood. Of course, the doctor wanted me to show him where I came from. Reassured, I gave a polite smile and lifted my finger, casting my eyes over the map. It was then that I felt my blood run cold. It was like leaning over the brim of an abyss. I recognized the shapes carved out on the map by the red scars of the frontiers, but I no longer knew what they were. The capital letters straddling valleys and mountains meant nothing to me. France, Germany, Austria, Hungary, Romania wandered around my mind as outlined shapes, but I could no longer put a name to them. Mentally, I could reach the threshold of those concepts, but then could find no handle to gain access to them. It was chilling to discover that half of my mind was clearly not under my control. It was as though the blood which should have bathed my brain had been left blocked in some distant and obstructed artery. When I tried to grasp them, ideas that seemed perfectly straightforward simply melted away before my powerless gaze. Even the letters, which I thought I knew one by one, which I had the feeling I could write without difficulty, had now become signs without sounds, mute hieroglyphics from some vanished civilization.

Then, urgent as a desire to vomit, I felt the sudden need to speak. Once again I had that feeling of obstruction. My head was spinning and I felt a shower of stabbing pains swarming behind my eyes like sparks. I opened my mouth, hoping to produce some sound, but all that came out was a gasp of air. I realized that my tongue, my mouth, my teeth were incapable of coherent speech. The air passed from my throat to my palate only to dissolve into a forlorn sigh. The horror of that dreadful discovery rooted me to the chair which I was clutching, my nails digging into its painted surface. I stared at the doctor in wide-eyed terror, hoping for help. My head was seized by the familiar swarming feeling, followed by the usual stabs of pain. I was prey to a fear such as I'd never known. I felt that I was sinking, losing all contact with the outer world. Here and there things seemed to be fading from sight, as though the faint glow lighting up the last narrow passageway between myself and reality was dying out. The doctor tried to conceal his dismay; he turned the map this way and that, keeping his finger pointing towards the outline of Finland. He let slip the odd word, an exclamation he repeated several times: for me these were just sounds, which I could hear but could not understand. For a moment, his expression seemed to betray the perplexity of someone who finds himself having to deal with a madman. The nurses rushed towards me to take me back to bed. Once again I felt something cold against my arm. The doctor stayed beside me until I fell asleep.

I opened my eyes again perhaps an hour or so later, too

exhausted to panic and too stricken to go back to sleep. The night-light in the corridor was flooding the walls of painted sheet-metal with yellow. The pitching, the black porthole, everything conspired to make me feel as though I were sinking slowly into a whirlpool, into a dark and cold abyss, peopled by monstrous fish. I felt weak, numb, unable even to cry. It was pitch-dark, both inside me and out. Grinding my teeth, I marshalled such rage as I could still summon up, and swore wordlessly at a God who could not hear me.

The next morning, Doctor Friari entered my cabin with a smile. The previous day's dismay seemed to have been forgotten, and he gave me a confident look. Under his arm he had a bundle done up in wrapping paper, and now I saw its contents for the first time. It contained a blue jacket, the kind that sailors wear. The doctor opened the package on my bed and showed me a bit of cotton tape sewn into the inside of the collar, with two words with capital letters written on it. I could make out the letters, but I was unable to read them. Doctor Friari was looking at me closely, and his expression was clearly intended to be reassuring. He had now begun to speak, his finger pointing at the label on the collar's lining. Stressing the initials, slowly he spelt out the words 'Sampo Karjalainen' with the metallic voice of an automaton. I tried hard to understand. I sensed that he was repeating what was written on the label. Standing in front of the porthole, he waved the garment before me, holding it by the shoulders. Thus taken hostage, the jacket seemed to take on a life of its own and struggle with the doctor, who had gone red in the face with effort. The sleeves flew upwards and then fell down again, as though inhabited by invisible arms, setting the buttons clicking. As though in some clumsy embrace, Friari passed his hands over the front of the jacket, looking for the pockets. He rummaged through one, then the other, and pulled out a folded handkerchief. This he opened up on the bed, letting the jacket fall to the floor. In one corner, embroidered in blue between blue lines, two letters stood out: S.K. I had no difficulty recognizing them: they were the capital letters of the name that appeared on the label. I could sense that the doctor was hoping for some reaction on my part. But, like the jacket lying on the floor, I too stretched out my arms in a helpless gesture, implying that I was beaten. My eyes were darting from the initials to the expectant face, the letters whirling in my mind, merging into a single indecipherable sign. Who was Sampo Karjalainen? Was I Sampo Karjalainen? Was that blue sailor's jacket mine? Overcome by hopelessness, I took my head between my hands, then let it droop until my chin touched my chest. I saw the doctor's shoes moving away over the wooden floorboards, then gliding towards the door. When I looked up, the blue jacket was still swinging slightly, now hanging from a hook in the wall.

I registered all the stages of that man's awakening from his coma with the utmost care. His blood pressure and temperature as they slowly rose, the first dawnings of consciousness, his gradual recovery of movement, everything was entered in his patient's file, together with the medicines I gave him. Even if I remember the order in which things occurred, much of what I wrote in those pages remains impenetrable to me. Often, adjectives and verbs follow one another in a succession of dry, bald words without any grammatical structure, stuck there like cut-out shapes. Rereading them, I could make some dim sense of them, I recognized the vague outlines of the sensations which that man felt and which I observed from the outside. I saw again the eyes which fixed me with such dismay, but I shall never be able to tell of the abyss from which they were surfacing.

A long time passed; the days seemed endless. Meanwhile I had recovered my sight. When they removed the bandages, I spent the whole afternoon looking at myself in the mirror screwed to the wall above the basin. At later stages, too, I often caught myself stealing a look at my reflection, trying to recognize myself. With the utmost caution, at times I would even venture delicately to feel the wound on the nape of my neck. But I was alarmed by the big hairless folds my fingertips would come upon amidst my ravaged hair. I skimmed over them with revulsion, as though touching my own brain.

With Doctor Friari's help, I had learned to whistle. This was a first step towards recovering my speech. The little military marches which I whistled were irresistible: indeed, I began to move in time with them. I spent whole afternoons doing the pronunciation exercises the doctor set me. Without understanding them, I had begun to utter my first words. As I began to learn more about my condition, I resigned myself and tried to cope with it with the means at my disposal. The doctor helped me to take my bearings in the sea of my unknown drowned consciousness. Thanks to him, I came to understand that I had a relatively extensive grasp of reality. From the windows of his office, where I would go each morning to work on my rehabilitation exercises, the doctor would point to some object in the landscape of the bay and ask me to draw it in his notebook. In this way I realized that I knew how a building was put together, how a lighthouse worked, how a ship was made. Doctor Friari would write the name of each object underneath the drawing and teach me how to pronounce it. I repeated the sounds I heard him say, hesitantly at first, then with ever growing confidence. They were becoming my words; I could repeat and read them on my own and, over time, I learned to put them together. Later, when I could answer the questions that were put to me, the doctor was able to map out my technical knowledge more accurately, asking me to give him information about the various images he showed me, sometimes by means of gestures. In other words, I found that I knew how a car functioned, that I could work a gramophone, use a monkey-wrench or screwdriver; furthermore, although I was unable to formulate it very precisely, I found that I was also in possession of a certain amount of nautical knowledge. My brain responded to the proffered stimuli, the current was getting through. It was just the switch of language which failed to function. But the emergency lead installed by Doctor Friari gradually made good this deficiency; however temporary and prone to leaps in voltage, it nonetheless managed to fuel my gradually redawning consciousness. My memory, on the other hand, was still shrouded in darkness, and no amount of seeking the point at which it had short-circuited would yield results. Of the flow of events which the doctor put before me with the help of photographs, maps and flags taken from his books, none served as an anchor for my identity. Here everything became a blur, slipping away as though shut off by clouded glass.

Accompanied by a nurse, I had begun to venture out on deck for the occasional short stroll, walking the length of the ship, holding on to the taffrail. Once I had reached the stern, I would sit down in the sun, facing the blue sea which for so long I had glimpsed only from the porthole. Later, I would learn that I was on board the German hospital ship Tübingen, riding at anchor off the Italian port of Trieste, waiting to unload its cargo of wounded so that they could be transferred on to Red Cross trains headed for Germany. On sunny mornings the distant city, dotted with green domes, seemed to be set upon rows of glittering waves, and I took pleasure just sitting and gazing at it. I felt reassured by that expanse of limpid water, that ordered countryside. On deck I also met other soldiers, thin-faced men with an absent air about them. All had some bandaged limb or were more or less obviously maimed. Some dragged themselves along leaning on makeshift crutches, which they still handled clumsily. Others seemed physically unimpaired, but on closer inspection turned out to have a bewildered look that was scarcely human. They gathered together in small groups, on the more sheltered benches, playing cards, chatting, or staring wordlessly into the distance, taking the odd puff of a cigarette. I tended to steer clear of them, since I myself had nothing to contribute. But when I caught some snatch of conversation I would eavesdrop, trying to make sense of the words I heard them utter. I would single out those I could hear most clearly, those they seemed to pronounce most often, and move away in order to repeat them aloud to myself. But those unknown sounds would echo emptily in my mouth and head without leaving anything behind, like an echo dying away gradually. At an unconscious level I felt that they were not those that figured in the language spoken by Doctor Friari. Even when I did succeed in reproducing them, they would melt away like bubbles without my being able to gain the knack of repeating them. I would go back to sitting alone, looking out to sea. But not even that majestic sight could calm my sense of dread. My gaze bore into the distance in the desperate hope of finding some foothold, some memory, some image which might miraculously bring the vanished part of me back to life.

Each morning after my walk, I would go to Doctor Friari for my daily session. Petri Friari – a neurologist at the university hospital in Hamburg – was a German citizen, but originally from Finland. As I was later to learn, he had fled his native land many years earlier, when he was little more than a boy. At first I had difficulty understanding his story, even though he had told it me on several occasions, aided by that same map of Europe and every gesture he could think of. It was not clear to me why he had left, but I sensed that his departure had tragic overtones. But, as I gained in understanding, as words proliferated in my mind, I managed to piece his tale together.

During the years when Russia was being riven by revolution, Finland too was caught up in the maelstrom. Workers in the industrial centres rebelled, took up arms and set up a communist government. The country split into two and civil war broke out, with the white armies commanded by Marshal Mannerheim emerging victorious after a long struggle. Once order had been restored, mercilessly repressive measures were taken against those who had sympathized with the Bolshevik cause. Doctor Friari's father, a university professor with socialist leanings, was arrested and sent to a prison camp. After the terrible winter of 1918, no more was heard of him. So Petri Friari, then a young medical student, had left Finland with his mother to seek refuge in Hamburg, to stay with distant German relatives. There, in order to survive, he had become a jack-of-all-trades, making huge sacrifices in order to complete his studies. He had not been back to his country since the age of twenty-three. But he had never forgotten his language; nor his people.

Backed up against the railway, blackened by smoke, the Gothic building of the Finnish sailors' church stands just outside the port of Hamburg, where the cranes thin out and the city dwindles away into grey countryside. There the doctor would meet up with fellow-Finns who had arrived by merchant ship; they would tell him the latest news, bringing him letters and newspapers. Every Sunday he would accompany his mother to mass, and spend some hours in the afternoon doing charitable work for the city's small Finnish community, whose members he would treat free of charge. In exchange he received warmth, affection and the occasional bottle of spirits, but above all the opportunity to speak his language, and it was this that he most welcomed. This was why Doctor Friari had taken such an interest in my case: the name embroidered on the label in my jacket was a Finnish name, and perhaps he saw my wretched situation as mirroring his own. I too had been unceremoniously flung out of my own country, and the language which the doctor believed to be buried somewhere in my damaged brain was also his. He cared for me and my wounds in the same spirit as he had tended to the sailors who frequented the church in Hamburg. During our sessions he would tell me about his past as though it were some sad tale whose ending he did not know himself, but which he enjoyed telling me, as though to ward off further misfortune. Welcoming me into his office, he would rub his hands as though in anticipation of some pleasant diversion. He would sit down and open his green notebook, which he constantly consulted as he told his tale, or questioned me.

Then he would show me pictures, different on each occasion, which were glued into his notebook or taken from some other book, and put names to them, asking me to repeat what he had said. The words he used were different from those I heard spoken by the soldiers on deck; at first I had difficulty pronouncing them; certain vowels I found particularly hard. But the doctor was wonderfully persevering. Later he told me that he himself was surprised at how fast I learned. A light dusting, a sprinkling of sounds had gradually settled on the smooth rock of my mind, becoming denser and more full-bodied over time. A rich, deep humus had formed, where words were now taking root and thriving. The linguistic memory which my injury had uprooted from my brain was being born afresh in another part of my mind, bolstered by reason but at the same time as spontaneous as a natural language. That was how the doctor put it, and indeed he was amazed that I could learn so quickly, drawing on mental resources which he had thought to be unsuited to the learning of a language. Secretly hoping to believe his own optimistic words, he ventured the fantastical hypothesis that my brain cells had tracked down the remnants of my language which lay scattered among the folds of my wound, and that the effort of learning had caused them gradually slowly to reknit, to take on shape and consistency. Some unknown chemistry was at work within me, new capillaries were branching out, bringing their juices to unexplored regions previously known only to the animal life of blood and flesh.

As he observed it, the doctor referred to this phenomenon as miraculous, and he took the greatest pleasure in all the stages of my progress. He noted down my reactions to his exercises in the greatest detail, together with the new words I was learning to use. He regarded my recovery as a personal triumph, a great step forward for science. But what he found most moving of all was the retrieval of a language which, in his own way, he too had kept safe within himself, ferrying it from exile into the seas of memory. Even though we could not engage in sophisticated conversation, and our dialogue consisted of single words, repeated to the point that they seemed almost to take on bodily form around us in the air, Doctor Friari felt that in some abstract way we both belonged to the same world. We were bound together by some mysterious link, some bond which was not to do with blood, but which resonated in the sound of language. In the doctor it revived the sweetness of memory, and in me it aroused the will to live.

I had been picked up on the verge of death, my head badly smashed, at dawn on 10 September 1943, on the quayside near the railway station in Trieste. I was not carrying any documents or personal possessions. All that I had was the clothes I was wearing. I had probably been attacked and robbed, hit on the head with the lead pipe found beside me, still daubed with blood and hair. During those same days the hospital ship Tübingen had arrived in the port of Trieste from North Africa, and it was to this ship that the sailors who found me belonged. They hoisted me on to their lifeboat and took me aboard, where I was put into the hands of Doctor Friari, a medical officer with the German navy. As he himself later admitted, in view of my serious condition, and the extent of my wound, he did not think that I had long to live; to the point, indeed, that he had not thought that it was appropriate to operate on me, so that he had accepted me on board the Tübingen for purely compassionate reasons, because of the name stitched into my jacket. But he immediately decided to have me transferred to the ward where the comatose wounded were admitted, and to keep me under observation in the recovery room. A large area at the nape of my neck had suffered deep lesions, and it was difficult to assess how much of my brain had been affected. But perhaps the doctor had sensed that something, somewhere within me, was still alive. As he later explained, clinically there was nothing to distinguish me from the other comatose wounded; whatever it was that had led him to tend me so meticulously, he saw as a nod from fate. As a man of science, practical and down-to-earth, he would come to see me each morning in the recovery room expecting to find me dead.

When he saw that in fact I was making progress, he scented a miracle: from that moment on, he never left my bedside. The day I came out of the coma, the nurses swore that they had glimpsed a tear on one of his far from tender cheeks. He insisted on taking personal charge of my rehabilitation; each morning it was he who put me through certain exercises using coloured cardboard cut-outs. When he realized that I could not speak, that the injury had destroyed my memory for language and my ability to articulate sounds, he hoped in his heart of hearts that I would die. Surprised at the speed with which my brain was retrieving lost knowledge, at first he was intrigued above all by the scientific aspect of my injury. But he could not remain untouched by the fear, the bewilderment of a man part of whom had been taken from him, a man deprived of his past, his name, his language, obliged to live without memory, nostalgia, dreams. The supposition that I too was Finnish, having ended up for some unknown reason in those distant seas, led him to care for me with a devotion rarely met with by the wounded in a time of war.

In the weeks he spent at my bedside, peering into my eyes for the least sign of consciousness, he had become convinced that I must indeed be a Finnish sailor, who had come to Trieste on board some ship, possibly a German merchantman; that I had then been set upon by one of the sharks who hung around port cities and railway stations in those war-torn times. The name on the jacket and the initials on the handkerchief left him in no possible doubt. So he swore that he would move heaven and earth to get me back to my own country, to give me the chance to pick up the broken thread of memory. After all, the very fact that I was still alive was at least in part his doing, for better or for worse. He had put his scientific knowledge in the service of blind fate, while his heart had been won over by the familiar sound of my name.

I waited on board the Tübingen for many weeks. Various problems had delayed the organizing of the troop trains to Germany. Now the ship was anchored in the port of Trieste. From my vantage point on deck I had noted frantic outbursts of activity on the shore and quays: military vehicles were arriving all the time, disgorging troops and weapons. When the wind was right, I could even hear the shouts of the commanding officers. Sometimes I would accompany the doctor to the station, where he would go to supervise the organizing of the troop trains or to procure medical supplies. On those occasions we would have lunch together, in some little restaurant near the port. As we ate, he would encourage me to tell him about everything I was doing, every detail of my day, even the most insignificant. At first I found this tedious, then I understood what he was aiming at. It was out of these spots of time that I would rebuild myself a past, a memory. He laid great stress on the importance of persisting with this exercise. Though he had not yet told me as much, the doctor was already mulling over a plan to get me back to Finland, and was slowly preparing me to make the break.

While the doctor was talking with his colleagues from the Medical Corps in the military quarters which I was not allowed to enter, I killed the time by taking walks. At first I did not stray far from the station, but later I began to venture into the city. On sunny afternoons, each street running inward from the sea was a gilded strip up which I walked as far as the shady squares further inland, where large buildings of white stone stood out against a deep blue sky. I enjoyed wandering at random, following the mirage which appeared beyond each corner and then emerging again into the blinding seaside light.

Those were months of deep uncertainty for Trieste. I knew that new German troops had come to occupy the city since the Italian armistice, preparing to fend off a possible landing. The German allies had become potential enemies. Many Italian soldiers had fled into the mountains, joining up with the partisan groups, or had already been disarmed. Black Shirts and Salo soldiers had taken up their posts, under the German command. Doctor Friari was wary of these men, not regarding them as soldiers like himself. I had noticed that he tried to avoid them, and above all that he treated them with hostility. In the last days before my departure, during my solitary ramblings, I would hear sudden volleys of sub-machine-gun fire breaking the silence of the almost deserted streets. I was even stopped by the occasional patrol. But my *laissez-passer* had invariably sent the arms of the officers who opened it into a smart salute. Their voices immediately changed, and they allowed me to proceed. In the station, no one stopped me watching the troop trains leaving for the Yugoslavian front. Often I would go and look at the place where I had been found, a few steps from the commercial quay. I would search among the cranes and anchored ships for some trace, some clue that I might transform into a memory. Sometimes, while I waited for the doctor who was dining with some high-placed officer, I would find myself in the city until late at night and, just for a bit of human company, would take refuge in the first bar I came upon. Here, amidst German soldiers and Black Shirts who were getting drunk and singing, I would nurse my small glass of beer for as long as I dared, singing songs I could not understand along with my unknown drinking companions. It was reassuring to hear my voice mingling with others, to hear my own words overlaying theirs, emerging from my mouth and springing into life as though they were truly my own, as though behind those sounds which I had learned to imitate so well there were also some awareness of their meaning. Without addressing a word to me, the men around me would raise their glasses, clink them with my own, treat me as one of themselves. In the fug and din of those bars I felt protected: I was not alone. My fear of loneliness worried the doctor. He said I must get over it: it was a sign of my inability to accept my new destiny.

One morning in November Doctor Friari asked me to go with him to the small town of Opicina, up on the Carso just outside Trieste. He had to go to the German headquarters to meet a high-ranking civil servant working for the civil administration who had just arrived in town. I was still unaware that it was I who was the object of this trip. A car came to pick us up on the quay. It was a grey morning, though to the east the light-filled sky promised sunshine. The road that led up to the Carso was shrouded in thick mist. The whole of the upland plateau was oozing moisture; every so often fat droplets fell from the trees on to the windscreen, like sudden summer rain.

The German headquarters were housed in a fenced-in villa with an imposing white gate, set back a little from the street. We crossed the gravel-strewn courtyard embarrassed at the noise of our own steps, to be met by a soldier who, I noticed, walked with a limp. He exchanged a few words with the doctor and led him towards a door at the end of the hallway, gesturing that I should go into the officers' mess, which was empty at that hour. I sat down and began to leaf through some old magazines. After long minutes spent in silence, I heard his limping step returning, then the door opened and the soldier appeared, beckoning me to follow him. I was escorted into the office, where the doctor and the civil servant were deep in conversation. The civil servant was solidly built, with a red face and a genial smile. He came towards me to shake my hand, gesturing towards an armchair in front of his desk. I sat down, and the doctor, seated beside me, carried on with a conversation which my arrival must have interrupted. He was speaking in German, but I sensed that it was my story he was telling. He pointed to the jacket, which I had taken off and was now holding folded on my knee. At a gesture from the doctor, I pointed to the label, brought the handkerchief with the initials out of a pocket and laid it on the desk. The civil servant turned it over in his hands, frowning, then handed it back to me. The conversation did not last long. The civil servant nodded as the doctor spoke, and took some notes. Then he stood up, took us to the door and bade us a warm goodbye. He also addressed a sentence to me personally in his warm, raucous German; I did not understand it, but sensed it was intended to be well-meant. The doctor, on the other hand, did understand, and shook the civil servant's hand, giving him a grateful look. I too thanked him, bowing my head in place of words. The lone soldier led us through the gravel-strewn courtyard to the gate. We waited for his limping step to die away before getting into the car.

Now the mist was clearing, rising hazily towards the woods. As we left Opicina flashes of sunlight were already visible over the rocky coast, falling on the sea and dispelling the last strips of cloud. At the first turn in the road the bay came into view, spread out in front of us. The doctor pulled the car to the side of the road; we got out and walked along a stony track running round the side of the hill. Even though the countryside was bright with the fiery colours of the woods, there was a touch of winter in the cold sky. In the deeper dips in the uplands, where patches of cloud still lingered, the trees were already bare. When we reached the top, we sat down on a low stone wall, looking out at the empty horizon and the city below us, set in the dazzling sea.

'In two days the troop train will be ready,' the doctor told me. He was gazing into the distance, trying to find words which I could understand. Raising his voice, as though hoping that it would penetrate more deeply into my mind, he went on:

'The time has come for you to face this journey. You must not be afraid. Basically, this journey is a return. Here you are living in a sort of limbo, a no-man's-land, your life is in abeyance. Do you understand me?'

I nodded, even though I had barely grasped the meaning of what he said. Looking out to sea again, the doctor went on:

'You must go back to your past life. Only there can you hope to find something that will jog your memory. Sometimes all it takes is some smell, some trick of the light, some sound that you have heard a thousand times, however unknowingly.'

Smell, light and sound, these had been the instruments of my awakening. The doctor fell silent for a few moments, giving me a conspiratorial look. I did not know what he was thinking, but I sensed that he would have liked to be leaving with me.

'Now you must start to learn your language. This above all will help you with your memory. The merest breath is enough, if there is still any fire at all beneath the ashes.'

Seeing my blank expression, he repeated what he had just said, miming the lighting of a match, the flame swelling, and rising.

'You'll see, it won't be difficult. But you will have to make an effort. You won't be able to make do with just a few words and the odd gesture, as we have done these past few weeks. You will have to work hard at your language. Finnish is the language in which you were brought up, the language of the lullaby that sent you to sleep each night. Apart from studying it, you must learn to love it. Think of each word as though it were a magic charm which might open the door to memory. Say each word aloud as though it were a prayer – prayers are made up of words. Turn over its every meaning, its every usage, in your mind.'

I frowned. I could no longer follow what he was saying, but I did not want to interrupt the flow. His words were music, and that music was about me. The doctor saw my difficulty, and tried to describe the more difficult concepts, once more with the help of gestures. Some words he could only uselessly repeat, breaking them down into syllables to show me the pieces one by one. To no avail, the meaning still escaped me; yet, though they dissolved like morning mist, those syllables were not entirely lost. Repeating them to myself I somehow captured traces of them and, much later, those fossil remains yielded up the doctor's thinking.

The wood around us was rustling with the faint sound of raindrops instantly drunk in by the earth. I felt I could hear the leaves shrivelling, as though all autumn were draining away in a few minutes. The doctor clasped his hands, trying in vain to find some way of communicating his feelings, his advice. Finally he spoke without caring whether I understood or not, in a sudden outburst, giving vent to an evident irritation that his words would simply be borne off on the wind.

'One more bit of advice,' he said. 'I speak now as a man, not as a doctor. Since language is our mother, try and find yourself a woman. It is from a woman that we come into this world, from a mother that we learn to speak. Fall in love, give of yourself. Switch off your brain and follow your heart. You must fall in love with a voice, and with every word you hear it utter.'

Perhaps because it was followed by a long silence, that

last phrase, without my understanding it, stayed in my mind. I repeated it, committing it to memory as a frozen block of sounds within which I could discern some meaning. Later, as it dissolved in my mind, I picked the words out of it, the most important last: *rakkaus*, which means love.

But the glorious landscape laid out before us, the glassy sea, puckered in the distance by the movement of the wind, and the sun, now hot in the still hazy sky, were not conducive to such weighty thoughts. Enchanted by that heartening view, we both fell silent for some time. Even the war seemed far away. From up there the city, so ill-at-ease and anxious, looked like a Christmas crib, and the warships criss-crossing the bay like so many toys. The doctor turned his face to the sun. I stared at the rock at my feet, dropping away steeply into the blue abyss of the sea, and pursued my thoughts. More than his words, which I had barely understood, it was the doctor's tone which had struck me. I sensed that some moment of truth was approaching, that I was moving towards an appointment I could not fail to keep. I had to solve the puzzle which had cut my life in two. Even if I was by now more or less accustomed to the atmosphere of that unknown city, of that ship anchored outside time, I felt that I could not stay there for ever. The slow-moving smoke from the odd chimney rose from the dazzling city at our feet, together with muffled sounds. As though he were reading my thoughts, the doctor said:

'And seeing that we are compatriots, when you get there, please send my old Finland my warmest greetings! These weeks of teaching you such little as I could remember of our language has been a voyage of discovery for me too. I have found words which had been forgotten in the cracks in my memory. When I was a child, my mother would often come out with the following saying: '*Oma maa mansikka, muu* *maa mustikk*a' (One's own land is like a strawberry, other people's is like a bilberry). *Mansikka* is the strawberry, red and sweet like our land. *Mustikka* is the bilberry, black and sour like other people's. In other words, everyone is best off in their own home. Who knows, perhaps my mother foresaw the fate awaiting me, and those words were a warning. Perhaps meeting you in this way in such a far-flung place is a sign, a message she is sending me from the other world to say that it is time for me too to go back home!' He gave a crooked smile, perhaps wanting to believe as much himself; he looked at me for a moment, then quickly turned his gaze in a less challenging direction, towards the distant sea.

The doctor had made the preparations for my departure. I would leave with the troop train that was taking the wounded from the Tübingen back to Germany; from Trieste, it would go to Dresden via Ljubljana, Vienna and Prague. From Dresden, I would carry on to Berlin and then Stettin, with a *laissez-passer* the doctor had obtained from the civil servant we had met in Opicina. From there I would be able to take ship for Helsinki. The doctor gave me several letters of introduction to be given to a colleague of his in the military hospital in Helsinki, in which he explained my situation and described the injury I had sustained.

'Ask for Doctor Mauno Lahtinen,' he said, making sure I had understood. 'He's an old classmate of mine from the time when I was studying at the University of Helsinki. We have seen each other only once over these last twenty-six years, at a neurologists' congress in Berlin, but we are in regular correspondence. I know that he is doing service at the main military hospital in Helsinki.' He also gave me the money for the journey, and for my initial expenses. He was insistent that I should not hesitate to mention his name if I had problems with the German authorities.

'If the worst comes to the worst, tell them to telegraph the Gauleiter of Carinthia, Doctor Friedrich Reiner, the man we met in Opicina. He knows all the details.'

A fine rain was falling on the morning I boarded the train to Dresden. The sky was full of billowing, low-lying clouds. Doctor Friari came with me to the platform. I sought for words of thanks, but could manage only to clasp his hand. He noted my emotion, but on this occasion contained his own.

'Courage! You are going home! *Oma maa mansikka ...*' At the moment of our leave-taking he assumed a soldierly indifference which he had never shown before. His last words were as follows:

'I hope you will be able to make a new life for yourself. Or find the one you lost. I will not ask you to keep in touch. I know that when you find peace and serenity you will not want to think back to these days. But at least, if you can, remember me. Being remembered – that is all we ask for, is it not?'

Drawing his overcoat around him, he said another quick goodbye as the train pulled out. I never saw him again.

Reading these pages, I felt deeply moved. Reflected in this narrative I glimpsed aspects of myself that were quite unknown to me. It contains almost all the words I spoke, and my own personal story sounds even more bitter as told here. Though he could speak no language at the time, that man could read into my silences, could sense my fear. I well remember our first meeting in my office, on board the Tübingen. Without realizing what I was doing, I had begun telling him my story. I was convinced that he could not understand me, and I was talking mainly in order to give vent to my feelings, something

I had never been able to do, not even with the sailors in the Hamburg church, for fear that someone was spying on me. I had not realized it, but my pain was so intense that it leapt clean over those words and straight into the heart of that man, whom I had treated like a deaf-mute. How he managed to articulate whole portions of my outbursts, I do not know. Luckily I still have the diary I kept during that time. The green notebook, as he called it. Alongside my personal notes, I registered everything significant that happened on board. That notebook has helped me to reconstruct the chain of events with considerable accuracy, and to recall our conversations. Above all in the first part, some passages of the document were hard to interpret, and I had trouble making sense of them. But, spelling mistakes apart, many of the sentences I used to tell my story are reproduced here with alarming accuracy, as though they had been learned by heart. So heavily had those words weighed on that man's mind that he had put his trust in me.

After long weeks spent off Cyrenaica, picking up the war-wounded from the fighting in Africa, my periodic returns to Trieste came as a relief. That light-filled bay gave me an illusion of peace; I had my feet on dry land at last. No longer haunted by a sense of danger, at night I finally found sleep, I had time to do a little reading, even to do nothing, if I so chose. I was drawn to that unforthcoming, foundling city. Neither Italian, not Austrian, nor Slav, it thrust its shameless beauty in my face, and I looked back at it a little shyly, as one might cast glances at a woman known to be unattainable. Sometimes I fantasized that I would stay there when the war was over. But I felt that it was too grand a setting for a life as colourless as mine. Those who live in such a city have an obligation to be constantly in love, because great joys, like great sorrows, demand grand backdrops. When the Tübingen, emptied now of its cargo of suffering and its stench of flesh, weighed anchor to sail northwards once more, the sight of Trieste receding into the distance brought with it an overwhelming sense of the most tender melancholy; parting is indeed such sweet sorrow. Once again I felt that I had missed an opportunity to embrace that city, and I imagined that perhaps, disdainful though she was, in some sense she too yearned for me.

The journey to Opicina on that autumn morning, over the Carso emerging from the mist, remains imprinted in my mind, together with everything I said, so I was able to reconstruct its gist. It was hard to find a way of making myself understood. We were dealing with concepts, ideas, and at that time the author of these pages had words for things, and things alone. Today I see, with some surprise, that he had retained my words until such time as he was able to decipher them. It is true, I too would have liked to have been sailing back to Finland; to take advantage of the chaos of war in order to do away with the neurologist from the military hospital in Hamburg and replace him with the Helsinki university student of twenty-six years earlier. But this was no longer possible. Twenty-six years do not go by without leaving their mark. Memory overlays itself like lava, causing recollections to be preserved, it is true, but also stealing them from us for ever. Memory, which the author of these pages was so wretchedly pursuing, still has me in its grip. Memory is the tithe of pain I pay, each day, when I wake up to this world and agree to live in it. Why, I do not know. Perhaps because it is easier to be born than to die; perhaps because of the unwholesome interest which all men feel in seeing how it will all end, whatever pain it may cause them.

I did not expect my arrival in Helsinki to be like this. I was not expecting that grey dawn, that threatening sky. The city which was coming towards me like a looming mass had nothing welcoming about it. The Swedish merchantman on which I had travelled, the Ostrobothnia, had turned its engines off. It pitched meekly amidst the slabs of drifting ice, its rusting prow pointing skywards. On the quay, silent men had picked up the hawsers from the muddy snow and were running to secure them to the moorings. The general mood was wary, watchful. Some soldiers had already come aboard and were looking idly into the hold, accompanied by a sailor. The captain, who had accepted me on board reluctantly, and only after the closest questioning, was smoking nervously, scanning the façades of the black buildings in front of the port. I thought back to the barracks at Stettin, the long line of soldiers walking, heads bowed, and the strange brightness of their new mess tins; that prying face behind the desk, my documents, leafed through times without number. Then the journey by lorry to the port, the rain-filled potholes, the jumble of wharves, and that suspicious look for ever trained on me, that mouth, shaped like a scar, opening every now and again, as though it were on the point of saying something, but then remaining silent.

'Where will you go, here in Helsinki?' it asked me, a butt-end clamped between its owner's lips. He had posed me the same question on the voyage a hundred times. Perhaps he was hoping to catch me out, to discover some inconsistency in my replies.

'I have the address of a military hospital; and a letter of introduction, from Doctor Friari,' I told him yet again, in my rough and ready Finnish.

'Anyway, wherever I go, it's all the same to me,' I added.

The officer shifted his gaze towards the city, turned his back on me and replied:

'This isn't just any city. It is an encampment of Mongols

who surfaced at the other end of the continent by mistake; savages whose only thought is to get drunk, even on ethyl alcohol if they can't find anything else!' Pleased with his words, he turned around and drew deeply on his cigarette.

'Welcome to Helsinki!' he added sardonically, then walked away, tossing the butt end into the sea. Perhaps he had had those words stored away for me right from the beginning of the voyage.

I walked away from the port with my knapsack over my shoulder. I felt a slight feeling of nervous excitement, but it was not unpleasant, indeed it was more like a kind of sharp and unaccustomed happiness. Walking in the tracks left by the lorries, between the piles of muddied snow, I felt that I was going to make the acquaintance of my own city, my own country, and that thought filled me with hope. A soldier pointed out the military hospital, on a wide street in the centre of town. I shook the snow and mud off my boots and found myself walking over a red-tiled floor, shiny with wax, and entering a tall, poorly-lit entrance hall. The nurse at the reception desk asked me a quick question which I could not understand. I answered by repeating the introductory sentence which Doctor Friari had taught me, and handed her the envelope marked with the seal of the Tübingen. The woman got to her feet and nodded to me to wait, pointing at the wooden benches against the wall; then she went off elsewhere. I removed my cap and took a deep breath of air, which smelled of a combination of paint and ether. Some petty officers came in through the main doorway and stood chatting in the hallway before going off down the corridor, their voices echoing until they died away behind some door. I listened to them with interest, as though amazed to hear them talking like Doctor Friari. So that was really it – the Finnish language at last, alive and well around me, filling that unknown space with sounds I knew. Within the network of my ear, straining to catch each syllable issuing from the mouths of those men, among so many that were unknown or mangled, certain whole words remained trapped, still living when I caught them. I held on to them, took them apart, compared them to those I knew, repeating them under my breath. They were real, they were already mine!

A soldier who had come to sit on the bench opposite mine now distracted me from my wandering train of thought. He had put his elbows on his knees and let his head droop. Eyes on the floor, he seemed to be following something moving in the geometrical design of the tiles, and every so often he would raise the tips of his boots as though to let something pass by. I noted that he was wearing a jacket like my own: the same dark blue, the same horn buttons, but with badges sewn into the collar. I stretched out my arms and looked at them. I stroked the rough material and thought, yes, this country must indeed be mine.

I did not have to wait long. The nurse appeared from a door opening off the corridor and ushered me into the out-patients' department. The doctor who received me had already read Doctor Friari's letter; he had it open in front of him on his desk. I sensed that his worry was how to make himself understood. When he began to talk, he pronounced each syllable unnaturally clearly, letting each word die away before starting on the next. This was helpful. From him I learned that Doctor Mauno Lahtinen, the hospital neurologist, was away at the front in Karelia, but he would soon be back, and would certainly take care of me. For the moment, all they could offer me was a camp bed and food from the soldiers' mess. The doctor repeated this last phrase in a different voice, perhaps for emphasis. These were words I knew, among the first I had learned on board the Tübingen. He added others which I could not grasp, but they cannot have been important, because he was already looking in another direction. Folding my letter back into its envelope, he put it into an unnamed file among the others heaped up on a cabinet behind him. The doctor noticed me casting a worried look in the direction of the still blank label on the sheet of grey cardboard, but he said nothing to reassure me. Then he stood up, to let me know that our interview was over, and shook me vaguely by the hand.

The nurse took me down the corridor to a large room whose walls were lined with shelves and white-painted cupboards, and handed me some rolled up sheets and blankets. I followed her again, this time through empty dormitories lit by large barred windows, then into a lighter corridor running around a courtyard, and finally into a slightly smaller room, where I counted six camp beds. She stopped at the foot of the last of them, handed me a key bearing the number six, and pointed to an iron trunk. She asked me something I could not understand, then waited for a moment for my answer. She smiled at my perplexed expression, then lowered her eyes, even more at a loss than I. When even the rustle of her uniform had died away, seated on the mattress of that unknown bed I felt all the silence, all the loneliness against which I had battled during my long voyage from Trieste to Helsinki, close up like water over my head. I was like one of those fishes left trapped by the ice under the Arctic sea. I could see light above me, but the call of the deep was stronger. I took off my shoes, somehow managed to cover myself up and fell asleep. It was weeks since I had slept in a real bed.

I was awoken by a bell whose sound seemed to be coming from outside. I had no idea how much time had passed. I heard steps in the courtyard outside the window, a vague sound of voices. I buttoned up the jacket I had not even bothered to take off, put my knapsack into the trunk and went out, following the sound of the bell, to join a queue of soldiers and nurses which was moving in the direction of a white church; on entering it, I saw that everything inside it, apart from the organ, was white too. The daylight was fading, and I could see red reflections of it on the glass of four skylights set into the ceiling. Three gilded numbers hung from a wall to one side of the altar. On the bench I found a missal bound in waxed paper, and a Bible with a red marker. There was a sound of rustling missals, and the singing began. A military chaplain walked up to the altar. He read out several passages from a large volume placed on a tripod; he was wearing a grey uniform, and his hair was so fair that it looked almost white. After he had read from it, he held each page of the book between his fingers before turning it gently over, a candle flickering beside him. The service did not last long, and was punctuated by fervent silences at the end of each hymn. I leafed through that strange Bible, looking from one line to the next, trying to recognize at least the names. I listened to my neighbours' singing, envious of those mouths so full of words. At the end of the mass, people filed out one by one, though some remained kneeling in prayer.

The smell of the wood and the wax had had a calming effect. I felt safe, out of the clutches of the captain of the Ostrobothnia and the metallic voice of the loudspeakers announcing each station's name; far from the carriages of the Red Cross train, from the smell of smoke and sweat rising from the endless soldiers asleep on their kit-bags. I too stayed in my pew, clutching that Bible as though to squeeze out of it the prayers I could not say. I felt besieged. Outside that church lay loneliness, and as soon as the last soldiers had filed out of its doors, that loneliness would seep in through the cracks in the wood, from under the door, through every chink and crevice; it would envelop me, sucking away my breath, but leaving me alive. My mind was running through doorless corridors, when I felt a hand on my shoulder and, turning round, recognized the nurse who had showed me to my room. She was with the military chaplain, who bowed his head slightly by way of greeting and said: *'Tervetuloa taloon!'* (Welcome home!)

This was how I met the Lutheran Pastor Olof Koskela, the only friend I ever had, the only person I now miss. He left for the Karelian Isthmus at the beginning of June and I have heard nothing of him since. A few days ago, a soldier from the twentieth regiment of frontier guards, wounded at Kuuterselkä, called out his name in his delirium. During all these months, not a day has passed without my being seated at the rough table in the sacristy behind the church, where Chaplain Koskela taught me Finnish with the patience that only a missionary can muster. Bent over an old yellowing notebook gradually filling with new words, day after day I learned what I believed to be my mother tongue, conjugating verbs and declining cases, reciting prayers, singing the hymns from the services and learning strange stories from the *Kalevala*. It is Chaplain Olof Koskela who has taught me to love this country. If he had had the time, he might have managed to make a real Finn of me.

Weeks passed, but there was still no news of Doctor Lahtinen. The nurse kept telling me that he was expected any moment, that he could not have been posted elsewhere because no replacement had been appointed. But I soon realized that no one at that hospital had time to devote to me. Those were terrible times for Finland. After the Winter War thousands of refugees had poured out of a ravaged Karelia; no one knew where they were to be housed. Those who could went to Sweden, to stay with relatives; others wandered from one train to another, ending up outside some village and building themselves a wooden shack in which to pass the winter. Many of the sick and elderly were taken temporarily into hospitals and assorted shelters; I was regarded as belonging to this category, and I paid for my bed and board by helping the nurses. But the doctors had other things to do apart from tending to my lost memory: there were the wounded and sick to be looked after, hungry people to be fed, children to be nursed through illnesses. It even occurred to me to wonder whether Doctor Lahtinen actually existed, or whether Doctor Friari had invented him, to reassure me, and that he had said as much in the letter I had given to the doctor on duty.

One morning, Pastor Koskela went with me to the War Office, in search of some clue which might help me discover my identity, but the staff had been transferred to safer places outside the city. The General Staff were said to be lying low in some bunker in Lapland; the archives were inaccessible. The sole employee we found in the empty rooms of that abandoned building clearly had other matters on his mind: perched on a ladder, he was clearing the upper shelves of a gigantic filing catalogue. He came down, somewhat unwillingly, and leafed through the registers of ships and those who had sailed in them, taking them from the crates where he had just placed them, and telling us brusquely that without the name of the ship or the date of recruitment he would be unable to give us any information. He advised us to talk to the Servicemen's Association, which had lists of the dead and missing. 'And anyway there's no saying that this is a naval jacket. It hasn't got the badges; it might be just something a sailor happened to be wearing!' he told us as we were walking away down the corridor, cluttered with trunks and dusty documents. We also went to the Central Registry Office, but the employee we spoke to made a despairing gesture when he heard my name. 'Half Finland is called Karjalainen! Without even a date of birth, where am I going to start?' he exclaimed despondently, gesturing towards the rows of numbered shelves behind him, bursting with files done up with string.

As time passed, though, all this began to matter less. The pastor became my family, the hospital visitors' quarters my home. Every so often I would be joined there by some officer who was passing through, though mostly all I would see of him was the rumpled bedclothes in the morning, or some vague outline under the sheets when I returned at night. I always came back late, because the quiet and loneliness of the visitors' quarters frightened me; loneliness had become my great bugbear. When I was alone, all the unanswered questions kept temporarily at bay by my fitful daily activities would come flooding back. For such relief was indeed only temporary: even if I deluded myself into thinking that I could bear it, the wretchedness of not knowing who I was, was gradually building up within me and sapping my strength; slowly and firmly, it was swelling to occupy the space that it deserved; for without memory, no man can live.

I would spend my nights in the lobbies of the larger hotels, the Kämp or the Torni for example, which were always crowded with journalists, soldiers and a motley cross-section of humanity at large. There, in the din and fug, anonymous among people unknown to me, I felt at ease. When even the bar in the Kämp emptied out, leaving only the odd waiter clearing up the ashtrays, I would go back out into the street and wander aimlessly through the city, or take refuge from the cold in the station, where I would watch the soldiers and evacuees arriving from the front. I would feel a gleeful shudder of apprehension when the carriage doors opened, and men with bloodied bandages and stricken eyes would step down on to the platform without any idea of where they were going to go. One by one I would look them straight in the eye, recognizing the same expression of bewilderment I had seen on my own face, reflected in the mirror, that morning so many months ago on board the Tübingen. If I heard cries for help, I would hasten to the spot, offer to help bear a stretcher, unload a crate, give my support to an elderly evacuee standing in tears beside his few worldly goods tied up like rags. But deep within me I was delighting in all that hardship. It was only fair that I should not suffer alone, that other people's desperation should prevail around me. I would return to the hospital only when I was thoroughly exhausted, certain that I would fall asleep the moment I lay down. Yet by dawn I would be awake again, would get up and go to light the stove in the chapel. Of course the few bits of wood available were not enough really to heat the space, but at least they would take off the night chill. When it was time for the service, a faint warmth would greet the figures who came in out of the darkness to kneel down on the benches. For reasons of economy, I would light the candle only when the bell stopped ringing. When the chaplain went up to the altar, I would take my place in what had become my own personal seat and lead the singing of the hymns, though without yet fully understanding the meaning of all those round, plump words. But I pronounced them confidently, as though they were my own. One by one, I would home into their meaning, take them apart, pigeonhole them. I was learning to use them outside the church, in my as yet rudimentary conversations with the pastor. Singing those words was my way of taming them. Since I could not ferry them to the shore of meaning, I

47

had to approach them cautiously, ensure that they would not slip from my grasp, be lost in the unbroken flow of the singing. When I was sure of their phonetic outlines, Koskela would help me copy them out: as a result, together with the columns of verbs and nouns, the pages of my notebook somehow also emanated music, as though the notes had mysteriously become fused with the letters. At the end of the service I would collect the missals, blow out the candle and enter the sacristy to say goodbye to the chaplain before going to the refectory, where a cup of milk and a piece of bread which tasted of resin awaited me.

I never became close to any of the other soldiers. I was afraid of not understanding what they said; above all, I did not want to tell my own story. So I would always sit alone, next to the window, looking out at the silver birches in the courtyard. I would spend the rest of the morning giving a hand to the nurses, the *lotta*. I had learned from the chaplain that the corps of nurses at the military hospital, with their grey tunics and white belts, were known as *Lotta-Svärd*. I helped them wash the sheets, boil up the bandages in drums of water, disinfect the surgical instruments. There was a mid-morning break; the nurses would make tea, and sit and chat. They talked quietly, rubbing their reddened hands over the rough cotton fabric of their uniforms. Those hands reminded me of something I couldn't quite bring into focus, something familiar and motherly; whatever it was floated, tantalisingly, just outside the reach of my consciousness. Only then, in the warmth of the laundry with its steamed up windows, lying on a heap of covers, did I feel sufficiently untroubled to find sleep. Cradled by the reassuring chatter of the nurses, I found that loneliness had no more power over me.

It was in the early morning, when there was more light, that the chaplain started to give me regular lessons. It was cold in the sacristy, and my hands would go numb; but the hymns warmed my heart, and when the temperature became truly unbearable the chaplain would open the door of a cabinet with glass handles, reach behind a pile of missals and pull out a bottle containing a white liquid. This, I learned, was called *koskenkorva* and was extremely strong. What was particularly magical about that little bottle was that throughout all those months it remained half-full, as it had been at the beginning, however much we sipped from it. This was the personal miracle worked by the Military Chaplain Olof Koskela.

That antidote against the cold was also very helpful to the pastor in his various asides, when he recited the poems of Yrjö Jylhä or told stories from Finnish mythology. The characters from the *Kalevala* came most alive for me when that bottle of *koskenkorva* was out on the table, together with our two thick little glasses. Then the chaplain's cheeks would flame, and the austere churchman would become another man: the abrupt priestly gestures would disappear, and his body would take on a strange bonelessness, like that of a puppet. His face, too, would crumple into grimaces I never saw him make when he was sober. I cannot comment on the words he used, but I also sensed that his pronunciation altered: slackened by alcohol, his tongue and lips could no longer keep the consonants in place, and the vowels flowed out in streams, barely regulated by soft movements of the glottis. In this way the pages of the old grammar book that the pastor had found for me were overlaid by a personal Finnish grammar of my own, eclectic and many-hued, ranging from hymns to military marches, from stories from myth to excerpts from the Bible, from feats of arms at the battle of Suomussalmi to Olof Koskela's own childhood memories, when he lived in the city of Vaasa.

The pastor was not just any common or garden Finn: he was part of the Swedish minority which had settled in Finland. He also had Polish ancestors, and perhaps that was why he regarded the Russians as a special threat. He had the deepest distrust for everything that came from the east, the wind included.

'The word east means nothing on its own. In our language you have to be more specific. *Itä* means the east in general, *Kaakko* means the precise point where the sun rises. If we have two distinct words for east in Finnish, it is so as to avoid having to use the same word both for dawn, and for the direction from which the Slav invasions come,' as he explained to me one day. He used the map on the wall to give me his own personal reading of the migrations which had peopled Europe, talking of Finno-Ugrians and Ural-Altaics as though they were friends known to him personally, as individuals. He would make the most far-fetched connections, unveiling secret plots and colourful intrigues which I, while knowing nothing about them, instinctively felt I should not take seriously.

'For example, do you know the difference between the Turks and the Japanese? None! They're both Altaic peoples! It's just that the Turks veered off to the left and the Japanese to the right! And they're both sworn enemies of the Russians. Together they could have held sway over Asia! Their great mistake was to run off, one here and one there, leaving a feeble trail of weak and scattered people in their wake. My goodness! If only the Seljuks had stopped in Samarkand! Today the Slavs would all be on the other side of the Urals, and Finland would extend as far south as Moscow, which was indeed a Finnic city! Because we Finns are also descended from the Altaic peoples! It was the Slavs who cut us off from our original stock by forcing us to migrate northward!'

Nor did the pastor restrict himself to ushering me down the winding lanes of Finnish grammar. Speaking a language all his own, seasoned with a wide range of gestures and images taken from his books, he also provided me with an equally original vision of the world. He too clearly relished our daily lessons, possibly because he had been a teacher before the war and could hardly believe that he now had a pupil all to himself, a school all of his own. The sacristy behind the church had become the pastor's own private educational establishment, a Greek philosophical academy transported northwards to the snow, where instead of sitting in the shade of an olive tree or on the steps of a temple, we would be stamping our feet because of the cold and sometimes be able to see our breath.

These pages also contain pencil drawings, unsophisticated but extremely elaborate and detailed. They are usually landscapes, though their locations are difficult to pinpoint with any precision. They would seem to be views of the military hospital, seen from the road; in one the church in the courtyard can be made out. Others are scenes from the Kalevala, *partly copied from the illustrations in Koskela's copy. Further on in the manuscript there are fewer drawings, as though the author had abandoned the pencil for the pen as he gradually acquired the ability to express himself in words. The pages which follow give an example of one of Pastor Koskela's language lessons. Never have I heard Finnish described so affectionately, so forcefully. Returning to my country after all these years, I found the language altered superficially, but basically unchanged. I went towards it as one might approach the object of some long-lost love, afraid, on reacquaintance, that I might regret the time and pain expended upon it, or, worse still, that*

I might realize that it had not been worth that pain. Instead, I discovered with relief that I was still in thrall to those chipped sounds, those words eaten away by ice and silence; that I was still able to free my mouth from the harsh grimace required by German and allow the soft, rich vowels of my own language to blossom from it. A learnt language is just a mask, a form of borrowed identity; it should be approached with appropriate aloofness, and its speaker should never yield to the lure of mimicry, renouncing the sounds of his own language to imitate those of another. Anyone who gives in to this temptation is in danger of losing their memory, their past, without receiving another in exchange.

One evening after mass the chaplain put many more logs into the stove than was actually allowed, and leant his feet up against it. He gestured to me to sit down on the bench beside him.

'This was how the *runoilija*, the old singers of the *Kalevala*, told their tales: facing each other, with the *koskenkorva* between them,' he began, placing the bottle from the cabinet with glass handles on the bench. Then he went on:

'A good song is a song that is soon done, one that does not overstay its welcome. It is better to stop in time than to be interrupted in full flow, they said. You who wish to learn Finnish should know this, because Finnish is one single, unbroken song. Finnish is a language which should only be sung, that is its true form, its morphology. To speak it is like the prose version of a poem. It is for savages who know nothing of poetry.'

He spoke, drank and refilled his glass; he seemed to be looking through it, holding it between two fingers like some precious phial. At times he would pause, clutch my arm, draw closer to me and mutter a sentence under his breath. Widening his eyes, he would look around him, as though trying to see beyond what was around us, as though hearing the sounds of a world from which we were debarred, which existed just a millimetre away from our own. I did not understand his every word, but I saw that he was happy to be speaking, and that was enough for me. It made me happy too.

'Like so many glass vessels, forms contain the liquid that is words, which otherwise would seep away, dissolving into silence. The forms of a language inevitably have repercussions upon the speaker, it is they which mould his face, his land, his habits, where he lives, what he eats. The foreigner learning Finnish distorts his own bodily features; he moves away from his original self, may indeed no longer recognize it. This does not happen studying other languages, because other languages are merely temporary scaffolding for meaning. Not so for Finnish: Finnish was not invented. The sounds of our language were around us, in nature, in the woods, in the pull of the sea, in the call of the wild, in the sound of the falling snow. All we did was to bring them together and bend them to our needs. When God created man, he did not bother to send any men up here. So we had to do what we could to struggle free of defenceless matter on our own. In order to gain life, we had to suffer. First came trees, lakes, rocks, wind. Becoming human all on our own was no joke. Finnish is a solid language, slightly rounded at the sides, with narrow slits for eyes, like the houses in Helsinki, the faces of our people. It is a language whose sounds are sweetish and soft, like the flesh of the perch and trout we cook on summer evenings on the shores of lakes whose depths are covered in red algae, the colour of the hunters' houses and the berries which bead from the bushes in summer. Finland is a cuttlefish bone, a great concave stone within whose sandy womb trees sprout like mould beneath the endless northern light. Nibbled away by ice and ground into thousands of tiny islands, this is the figure that it cuts on the map next to plump Russia and bony but sturdy Scandinavia. Finland is what remains of something else: take away the Slavs, the Scandinavians, the Orthodox, the Catholics, the sea salt, the birch forests, scrape off a few hundred thousand tons of granite and what you are left with is Finland. If you were once Finnish, at some point or other you will find all this within you, because all this is not stored in your memory, it cannot be mislaid. It is in your blood, your guts. We are what remains of something extremely ancient, something which is bigger than ourselves and is not of this world.'

As suddenly as he had began to talk, Koskela now fell silent and settled back into his seat. Abruptly, the silence of all the woods of the north now fell upon the church. The stove was sending out a red glow, sculpting his face out of the darkness. Beyond the glass of the skylights, darkness was pressing down, creaking like the ice against the walls of the houses. Once more the same miracle had occurred: there on the bench in front of me, the bottle of *koskenkorva* was yet again half full.

Almost three months had passed since my arrival in Helsinki, and I had stopped asking about Doctor Lahtinen. The chaplain himself had made it clear to me that such inquiries were pointless. Perhaps he had been transferred, perhaps he really was in Karelia, perhaps he was dead. Perhaps he did not exist, as I continued to think, though without saying so. At all events no one had the time to look for him. With the bombing that was going on, the hospital staff had other fish to fry. The Russian planes would arrive by night; we could hear their distant rumble, the sound of the exploding bombs which they often also dropped over Vuosaari by mistake. Each raid would last for hours. People would leave the city or seek safety in shelters. No sooner had the sirens ceased their howl, than the first ambulances would arrive in the courtyard, and with them the first news of what had been hit, and the number of people who had died. *'Satama, satama!'* The port, that was the word I heard repeatedly. The Russian air force was targeting the heart of the city, where people lived, and it was human flesh which flew into the air.

More snow had fallen during those same days. It had settled nonchalantly over that landscape of death, giving the Finnish people the hope that the bad weather might prevent the Russians from attacking. But a few nights later a low moon rose up from the bay, lighting up the city as mercilessly as a beacon. Where the Russian bombs fell, the white mantle of snow would be rent apart, leaving long ribbons of mud and stones. Now I could no longer sleep at night. Stretched out on my bed, I would wait for the sound of the sirens; then I would join the pastor and we would go and find the people who were proceeding in an orderly fashion towards the shelters. Sometimes, in the weak light of the bulb hanging from the low ceiling, Koskela would carry on with his Finnish lessons even there: amidst the pervading fear, they would take on a positively apocalyptic tone. I became aware that he was not addressing himself to me alone, but to all and sundry, because the people huddled all around us could hear him too. Sometimes, trying to distract themselves from the sound of the explosions which shook the ground beneath us, they too would begin to listen in fascination to the weird ramblings of that half-Swedish priest who had his own very personal ideas about language and history.

I found his words both complicated and intriguing; each day they bound me ever more closely to my new (or old?) identity.

'When you are learning a new language, the first thing you learn is the noun; the word noun is associated with the word name, and naming a thing means knowing it. This is why we cannot pronounce the name of God, because it would be presumptuous to hope to know Him. The noun suggests an idea of something, it helps us know it. In Finnish to know is *tietää*, and *tie* means road, or way. Because for us Finns knowledge is a road, a path leading us out of the woods, into the sunlight, and the person who knew the way in the olden times was the magician, the shaman who drugged himself with magic mushrooms and could see beyond the woods, beyond the real world. It is of course true there is more than one possible path to knowledge, indeed there are many. In the Finnish language the noun is hard to lay hands on, hidden as it is behind the endless declensions of its fifteen cases and only rarely caught unawares in the nominative. The Finn does not like the idea of a subject carrying out an action; no one in this world carries out anything; rather, everything comes about of its own accord, because it must, and we are just one of the many things which might have come about. In the Finnish sentence the words are grouped around the verb like moons around a planet, and whichever one is nearest to the verb becomes the subject. In European languages the sentence is a straight line; in Finnish it is a circle, within which something happens. In our language every sentence is sufficient unto itself, in others it needs surrounding discourse in order to exist, otherwise it is meaningless.'

Oddly enough, when he gave me lessons during our enforced stays in the air-raid shelters, the pastor would not hesitate to launch into some almost dangerously liberal analysis of languages and people, without worrying in the least about divulging his personal ideas concerning good and evil. His sermons, on the other hand, were always very decorous and unimpeachable in terms of dogma; when he was preaching he did not make so bold as to divert the course of migrations, nor did he follow shamans into forests. When he was at the altar, Koskela was a different man: he closed ranks with his church and his sermons took the form of simple moral precepts, hand-me-down phrases which he uttered with a hint of tedium, as though he were acting a badly-learned part in a play he didn't much like. All that remained of his exuberant personality were the sweeping, tragic gestures, his way of sending his hands flying upwards, fingers outstretched. When he talked of God, he reverted to the familiar tone he used when discussing Ural-Altaics; but only someone who knew him as well as I did could have noticed. He always seemed to be in a hurry to bring matters to a close, not because he had some other duty to perform, but because for him everything had to be concluded as quickly as possible; as though life were a warehouse to be cleared, a lorry to be unloaded – a corvée like any other in the perpetual motion of the universe. Despite the fact that war and devastation were tightening their grip upon the city, the hours that I spent with Koskela were always utterly serene. We did not know it, but cutting ourselves off from the world during that endless winter was the saving of us. Trapped beneath the ice, harm was powerless against us.

'As long as it's snowing, they can't fight!' the pastor would say resignedly, looking out of the sacristy window. We were both looking forward to the thaw, although for different reasons: he because he may already have known of the death which he was going to meet and which, like everything else, he simply wanted to be over and done with; I because I cherished the fond hope that the part which had died within me might reawaken with the spring. As soon as I was out of his company I was again assailed by all the desolation which had dogged me since my reawakening on the Tübingen. I was beginning to be able to express myself, even if somewhat stiltedly. I would learn the words already declined, a different one for each case, and when I did not know how to put them together I made do with saying them at random, hoping that intonation and gesture would go some way towards making up for lack of syntax. And yet, while still lacking firm banks, the Finnish language was gradually carving itself out a bed in the quicksands of my mind, with the words that I had tamed coursing down it and gradually informing me of the meaning of others. Branching out and joining up, they sent the thousand drops of sound which make up a language into circulation, watering and strengthening my awareness, my ability to sense the boundaries of meaning. But I was still haunted by my ignorance of my own past. Wandering around Helsinki, I would sometimes be jolted by a fleeting sense of memory: the view from a corner of the street would suddenly seem familiar, and then I would set to scouring every foot of road, peering at the names on bells on the doors of the buildings to see whether there might not be some Karjalainen among them. I would dream that I was outside my old house, that someone up there was waiting for me, gazing nostalgically at an old photograph which had been slipped into the glass of the dresser. We had mingled but not totally bonded, Finland and I; something in me remained untouched by this mingling, as though deep down some buried identity was refusing to be wiped out and was struggling furiously to rise to the surface.

These are the clearest pages in the document. Koskela had evidently lent a hand in the drafting of these memories, which were probably put down on paper a long time after the author's arrival in Helsinki. Some sentences have corrections in a different hand, or are recopied correctly beneath the original. The frequent exercises in inflection and breaking down into syllables of the nouns subject to vowel-change, interspersed throughout the text, bear witness to the perseverance and tenacity with which the author studied the Finnish language, at least during the time the pastor was at his side.

A few days ago, Miss Koivisto suggested that we visit the air-raid shelter where the hospital staff would take refuge during the bombardments. I too was interested in seeing another of the places mentioned in the manuscript, in the vague hope of finding some trace of its author. We turned off the road and found ourselves in a dark space, littered with lumps of plaster and broken glass. Purely by chance, my torch picked out various names and bits of writing carved into the black tiles on the wall, and I suddenly felt deeply unsettled, my instinct telling me that I should instantly look away again. And yet, deep down, some deeply buried compulsion drove me to read each and every one of them, as though they might contain some secret. It was climbing the stairs, back into the white light of the road, that the memory flashed into my mind, that on the other pavement I suddenly recognized the barracks to which my father had been taken the evening they arrested him at the university. In my mind's eye I saw again the ill-lit parlour, the guards standing around it, the wooden plank beds carved with threatening words, recently gouged resentfully out of the

dressed wood like so many wounds, and my father looking at
me wordlessly from the other side of the grille. It was meant
to be a reassuring look, it was an attempt to inspire trust, but
in fact that mask of bogus confidence would sometimes slip,
leaving me alone, exposed to the full weight of his own fear.
That was the last time I saw him; and, as though I knew as
much, I remember how determined I was to slip my fingers
through the mesh of the grille for one last clasp of his hand.

Dusk came early at that time of the year. The snow was not
enough to light up the empty city, barred and bolted as it was,
with all the windows dark. The main monuments, caged in by
wooden beams, were reminiscent of the catafalques of some
forgotten religion. The buildings in the city centre were empty,
the ministries and government offices deserted, having been
transferred to underground premises out of town. Although it
was not yet at war, Helsinki was a city in a state of siege; the
only people in its streets were hurried civilians and drunken
soldiers. Fear oozed into the city from the frozen bay, lapping
at the streets and squares. Death entered it with the trainloads
of refugees, and spread throughout the smoke-filled lairs
where the few remaining inhabitants had taken refuge. There
was feverish talk of the latest news from the Russian front, of
the siege of Leningrad, of the railway at Murmansk which no
one had the courage to blow up. Some people cursed the war;
the future seemed to be closing in on all sides, like the horizon
around us. Each day seemed likely to be the last. This sense of
doom was at its most tangible in the fug of the press-room in
the Kämp, where I would take up my position in an armchair
by the bar, among people I did not know. Together with the
book of grammar Koskela had lent me, I would open up my
notebook and start copying out words from the newspapers,

Diego Marani

while listening in on the conversations going on around me. Whenever some important army officer or civil servant entered the room, a small knot of journalists would suddenly form, shouting out questions and leafing through their notepads. I would slip in amongst them, listening to each question as though it were the one I myself would have liked to ask and staring firmly into the eyes of the person being questioned while he gave his reply. Although I had only the barest grasp of what was being said, I laughed along with the reporters, and shook my head to indicate that I shared their irritation when the replies were too evasive.They offered me cigarettes and glasses of brandy, which I accepted without a word of thanks, as though they were my due. When the hubbub died down and everyone went back to their seats, I too would settle down on a nearby sofa, open the *Helsingin Sanomat* and pretend to read.

It was in the Kämp that I finally became friendly with a German journalist, although perhaps he was rather an acquaintance than a friend. We would greet each other and sit together without speaking, as though we had no need of words to understand each other. He must have pieced together his own version of my story from the few words we had actually managed to exchange. I knew that he was a journalist, and that he was German: that was enough for me. Hearing him talk his language, on the telephone or with some diplomat, I was reminded of the weeks I had spent on board the Tübingen, of the merciless blue of that sea, so different from the desert of ice that lay before Helsinki, of the radiant vision of Trieste and the kindly attentions of Doctor Friari. Since any attempt at conversation required an extreme effort, we had tacitly decided to abandon any further deepening of our friendship. After all, in that doom-laden atmosphere nothing seemed to have a future and friendship, like love, served merely to pass

61

the time. For me, not having to talk was always a relief; but his presence reassured me, gave me a sense of warmth. I would pretend that I had ended up sitting beside him by pure chance; with my notebook, pencil and newspaper, I liked to imagine that I too was a journalist, but I kept this piece of make-believe to myself. He would glance at me out of the corner of his eye, and seemed to have understood everything about me. One night the lobby of the Kämp was strangely deserted; he was sitting typing in a corner, next to the piano, I was in an armchair trying to put off the moment of returning to the hospital for as long as possible. I had drunk and smoked too much and was about to fall asleep, when I heard him whistling a tune which I must already have known. Without realizing it, I began to sing: *'Davanti un fiasco di vin, quel fiol d'un can fa le feste, perche xe un can de Trieste, e ghe piasi el vin!'* He turned round, intrigued, breathing the smoke from his recently discarded cigarette out through his nostrils. I raised the empty glass I was still holding and repeated that one verse of a popular drinking-song I'd heard so often in the beer-houses in Trieste. Smiling though disconcerted, the journalist offered me a cigarette and made some surprised comment in German. I shrugged, pointing to a print of a ship which was hanging on the wall. From then onwards he took to calling me 'Trieste', and that was how he introduced me to his colleagues. He had realized that I was not in fact a journalist, but apart from some vague questions about Trieste, he had never asked me anything. He observed and respected the mysterious notebook in which he saw me scrupulously taking down the words I would underline in the *Helsingin Sanomat*; without guessing the secret thread that ran between them, he had nonetheless sensed that they were not taken entirely at random. Seeing that I spent most of my time wandering around without anything to do, at first sporadically but then increasingly often he began to use me as an errand boy, sending me to the post with telegrams, to the Hotel Torni to pick up messages or buy him a newspaper, rewarding me with the odd mark and the occasional cigarette. He made his requests known to me by means of an extremely effective range of gestures, backed up by his personal brand of international German: *'Trieste, bitte, telegramm presto zum Post!'* he would say, without taking the cigarette from his mouth. When he left for the front at the beginning of June, other journalists employed my services. So, as time passed, everyone at the Kämp knew me, even though they knew nothing about me. The Kämp had become my home from home; I felt less anxious there, and my jacket was just one blue sailor's jacket hanging among others.

New Finnish Grammar

'They're looking for people to help with the bonfires. Tonight's the night.' I was the only person in the room, lying stretched out on my bed and staring at the ceiling, but the pastor had come into the visitors' quarters on tiptoe and had spoken in an undertone.

'The bonfires?' I asked.

'The army's putting great piles of wood together to the north of the city. Tonight, when the Russian bombers come, our men will set fire to them. It's a trick: they'll think they're seeing Helsinki going up in flames, and that's where they'll drop their bombs!' he explained, taking my jacket off the nail and throwing it towards me.

We piled into the lorries, which then drove off, lights dimmed, towards the forest further inland, along a track of frozen snow. It was pitch black; the snow gave off no reflection, and the dark sky loomed above us. Suddenly we stopped, deep in the woods; the whole column waited in silence, scanning the sky. I couldn't see hair or hide of the pastor, but I sensed that he was near me; I recognized the unmistakable smell of his overcoat, which smelt of musty paper, as did the sacristy. We carried on walking until we came to a large clearing, where groups of men were already at work around large heaps of cut-down trees; there were also several tractors, and dray-horses. The lorries drew up in a circle; we clambered out and formed a line, to be handed axes and saws. Then we were divided into teams, and each was given a task. I worked for hours in silence, unable to make out the faces of my companions. I recognized them by their movements, by the way they walked across the snow. The pastor was wearing a cap with the earflaps unfastened, so that they swung around with his every movement, making him look like one of the magicians from the *Kalevala* that he would show me from his illustrated version. Our team's task was to drag the trunks into the clearing after they had been cut down and roughly trimmed by other soldiers in the forest. We would saw them up into bits, then another team would come to collect them and pile them up. The exhaustion, the sweat, that whole clearing swirling with the men's white breath, those bodies working in silence, all gave me a sense of peace, of harmony. I was no longer alone, no longer an outsider. I was among my own people; I was working with them to protect our land. It was a powerful feeling; it lent strength to my right arm as I drew on the great toothed blade which bit so effortlessly into the flesh of the wood, as though it too was eager to bolster that surge of concerted energy. The pastor must have noticed, because he came up behind me and slapped me on the shoulder. The earflaps swung around, and I could imagine the expression on his face, although I couldn't see it. A whistle halted us in our tracks; the tractors turned off their engines and we all ran into the woods, then waited in silence. Shortly afterwards we heard a rumble, followed by several explosions: they were bombing Helsinki. Orders were barked out; a tanker emerged from the woods and began to douse the piles of wood with naphtha; the lorries formed into columns, in preparation for departure. I followed Koskela's earflaps, then found myself seated next to him, puffing and sweating. No one said a word; the only sound was my companions' laboured breathing. The column started up. Before we turned into the woods, a gigantic burst of flame lit up the whole clearing, then bounded skywards. Suddenly the faces of my companions leapt out of the darkness, each with its own fear, its own amazement.

We did not make for Helsinki, but headed north-west. After some time the whole column drew up on a road in the woods, and waited; a sergeant handed out cigarettes, and passed round a bottle of *koskenkorva*. Most of the soldiers had climbed out of the lorries and were listening to the sound of the bombs, trying to work out where they were falling. Then suddenly we heard the sound of an approaching rumble, increasingly clear, and loud. The Russian planes were right above our heads, we could almost hear the throb of the pistons, the metallic whirr of the propellers. The ground was shaken by several powerful explosions; the soldiers were becoming uneasy, some were running along the column looking for officers. Then the rumour spread.

'It's working!' someone shouted.

'Hurray!' we all shouted back.

Then the sound of singing rang out through the dark woods: voices previously held in check were now set free to rise upwards, soft and buoyant. It was as though all Finland were singing, as though the same song, delicate as glass, was rising from each woods, each lake, each far-flung house of that vast land. Restrained and gentle as it was, it seemed ill-suited to that night of war; and yet, ever more solid, ever more convinced, it flooded every last corner of the forest, leaving no place or heart untouched. Behind us the sky was aflame, the Russian bombers were flying above our heads but did not see us, and we, bareheaded now, beneath them in the woods, were singing: ever more loudly, louder than the planes, louder than the roar of the lorries as they moved off again, and our voices rose to a shout, our song became a battle cry. Now the rattle of bombs was all but drowned out by the sound of a marching song, its rhythm marked by the stamp of our heavy boots upon the ground. We were no longer afraid of being taken by surprise, indeed we wanted them to hear us, we wanted to fling those words of strength and outrage in their faces. I didn't know them well, but I managed to grasp the drift of those songs and imitate their sounds; I opened my mouth as though to drink in the music which was pouring down on me, fully to share the magic of that rhythm. The tune throbbed around me as though it were in my very veins, and even the distant flames seemed to move to its racked dance.

It was dawn by the time we were back in the city. We knew that Kotka had taken a bad hit, but Helsinki had been left relatively unscathed. There were a few hours until the morning service, but both Koskela and I were too excited to think of sleep; instead, we retired to the sacristy and allowed ourselves the luxury of burning a few large logs, and making tea. The room was filled with the fragrant scent of woodsmoke.

'Fire! Iron and fire! These are the only things that count in war! You whose name is Sampo – did you know that you are born of fire? *Sampo* is a sacred word for the Finns; the whole of the *Kalevala* revolves around it. No one can say exactly what it was, no one has ever seen it, because it has been destroyed. It might have been the pillar which held up the earth, and whose collapse for ever cut us off from the place we came from. Legend has it that the *Sampo* has three lids, which are made from the tip of a swan's wing, the milk from a barren cow and the seed from a head of barley. It could have been made only by Ilmarinen, the smith god who had already forged the 'lid of heaven', together with the planets and the stars. The queen of Pohjola had promised her daughter in marriage to the *runoilija* (poet) Väinämöinen, if he procured the *Sampo* for her. He gave the offer close consideration: the queen of Pohjola was the powerful ruler of the land of ice, and her people had tried to invade the fertile plains of Kaleva on more than one occasion; marriage with the daughter of his longstanding rival would at last bring peace to the two peoples. Furthermore, a young princess would give new life to his old blood, sapped by the passing of the years. The great *runoilija* wanted to ensure a radiant future for his people; for their sake he was even willing to forego the *Sampo*. So Väinämöinen instructed Ilmarinen to go to the kingdom of Pohjola, to render this great service to the queen of the land of ice. The faithful Ilmarinen obeys the orders of his lord. Arriving at the court of Pohjola he promptly sets to work, and on the first day the breath of his bellows coaxes into life a golden arch with a silver apex. it was most beautiful, it was prodigious, but it was not what he wanted, and the smith casts it back into the fire. The next day what he produces is a boat, completely red but with a golden stern and copper rowlocks, and clearly this is not the *Sampo* either. The smith persists: after drawing a golden-horned heifer from his forge, its forehead strewn with stars and the disc of the sun upon its head, and a plough with a golden ploughshare, a copper shaft and a silver tip, at last, on the fourth day, it is truly the *Sampo* that emerges from the flames. Ilmarinen is exultant: he places three mills beside it, one for making flour, one salt, and one gold. The magical *Sampo*, which will give men light, has been created. As a reward, the queen of Pohjola will offer her splendid daughter in marriage not to Väinämöinen, but to Ilmarinen. For this powerful ruler had already understood that Väinämöinen was a man of the past, from the time when the world was made of water and men were fish. The future lay in iron, and in the fire which melted it, turning it into the magical

Sampo!'

'So, do you sense the power, the truth that lies within this story?' the pastor asked me as he poured the tea.

I took the cup from him, my hands still red with cold. I had grasped the bare bones of it even if much escaped me, above all those strange words, those fantastical objects whose shape the pastor outlined vainly with his hands: I had never seen anything like them. But I had been captivated by seeing the sounds forming themselves in his mouth, to be turned into words, then melt away. When I could not understand them, I listened to them like music, a fascinated witness to their fleeting life. How many words were needed to bring a man to life!

Meanwhile, a smoke-laden warmth had built up in the church. Hanging above the stove, Koskela's overcoat and my jacket were drying, giving out a smell of naphtha. Without caring whether I was following or not, the pastor had begun to speak again.

'When you can read the *Kalevala* you will be a real Finn; when you can feel the rhythm of its songs, your hair will stand on end and you will truly be one of us! Look!' he added, opening the black leatherbound volume on the table. 'These are not just words! This is a revealed cosmogony, the mathematics that holds the created world in place! Ours is a logarithmic grammar: the more you chase after it, the more it escapes you down endless corridors of numbers, all alike yet subtly different, like the fugues of Bach! Finnish syntax is thorny but delicate: instead of starting from the centre of things, it surrounds and envelops them from without. As a result, the Finnish sentence is like a cocoon, impenetrable, closed in upon itself; here meaning ripens slowly and then, when ripe, flies off, bright and elusive, leaving those who are not familiar with our language with the feeling that they have failed to understand what has been said. For this reason, when foreigners listen to a Finn speaking, they always have the sense that something is flying out of his mouth: the words fan out and lightly close in again; they hover in the air and then dissolve. It is pointless to try and capture them, because their meaning is in their flight: it is this that you must catch, using your eyes and ears. Hands are no help. This is one of the loveliest things about the Finnish language!'

Koskela would intersperse his speeches with long pauses, during which he would become suddenly motionless, as though entranced by his own train of thought. This gave me time to gather up such scattered remnants as I had managed to grasp and put them down on paper. Sipping my tea, I would leaf through the pages of the *Kalevala*, seeking out the words which I did not know but which I had heard in his account, so that I could ask him about them. I would also linger on the images. I noticed that the signs that gave physical shape to that ancient language seemed to have something in common with the characters described: drawn in Indian ink so that they looked almost three-dimensional, the tousle-headed heroes had nothing with which to express themselves except the words that lay around them: solid and dense, these words marched across the page in geometrical, almost military order, reinforced by the alternating rhyme schemes. I did not read the rhyme, rather I saw it, like reassuring embroidery made of the same three letters, bonding the lines together like an iron nail.

My own personal knowledge of our national epic has enabled me to reconstruct some illegible parts of the preceding text.

The author was probably copying out sentences dictated by the pastor during his lessons: clearly, in his excitement, Koskela must have been speaking too fast for his still inexpert pupil to take them down in their entirety. As to Koskela's dense reflections on language, here and elsewhere, I have been able to reconstruct them thanks to the substantial notes written on the back of the illustrations in his copy of the Kalevala, *which I came across together with this manuscript. In an envelope glued into the jacket flap, along with sacred images and old Russian stamps, I also found various theological writings, indeed virtual dissertations, by the pastor which I incorporated into the manuscript where I felt that the author's notes seemed to be referring to them. I too would have liked to have known the Army Chaplain Olof Koskela, and to have talked with him of the* Kalevala *and of God. His reflections often surprised me: if in some places I recognized the signs of his religious training, others were marked by an open-mindedness rare in a Lutheran Pastor. I do not know how old he was, but judging by the date of his edition of the* Kalevala *I inferred that he was just a little younger than my father; so that I cannot help wondering which side he was on during the civil war. His dislike for the Russians is only part of the story. Perhaps Olof Koskela was indeed a shaman; certainly he was one of the few remaining free spirits in this country at the time.*

The pages which follow reproduce a series of dialogues; they are among the most indecipherable in the manuscript, full of crossings out, spelling mistakes and words in the wrong case. Sometimes it is not even clear who is speaking, and the responses are often incomplete, full of blank spaces. Clearly, this part of the manuscript was never corrected by the pastor, and I have been able to fill in the blanks with help from Miss Ilma Koivisto, indeed it was she who transcribed them. It was she who reconstructed the author's descriptions of the landscape, and other of his thoughts. In the manuscript text the digressions which introduce and follow the dialogues are only roughly sketched in, barely hinted at by fragments of sentences, single words, heavily rewritten or underlined. Like buoys on the ocean of the page, they pointed me towards the flotsam and jetsam of conversations I had had with the author on board the Tübingen in the autumn of 1943. In this way, encrusted now with shells and overlaid with seaweed, the thoughts of which I am once more taking possession do indeed belong to me.

It was snowing heavily as I left the hospital, one evening in late March. Walking as fast as I could along the Esplanadi, I heard what I thought was the sound of a piano playing, borne on a gust of wind, coming from the Kämp. Opening the door, I was met by the welcoming sight of a choir of uniformed nurses, standing before an audience that was, for once, quietly attentive. Shaking the snow from my coat, I too joined the crowd, taking my place in one of the back rows. The room was brighter than usual; there were lamps on the tables I'd never seen before, and various ornamental plants had been laid out at the foot of the little dais, itself covered with a red cloth bearing the emblem of the *Lotta-Svärd*. The piano had been moved into the middle of the room, and was being played by an officer from the frontier guards, who was wearing a uniform which was too big for him. The occupants of the front rows were mainly officers in regimentals, and ambassadors in tails; behind them sat the journalists, together with a group of soldiers wearing dark grey uniforms, with badges which I did not recognize, their chapped faces suggesting that they had just returned from the front. It was beside one of these that I had seated myself; he was listening to the choir as one hears mass, with his head bowed and his hands placed firmly on his knees. The red mark of a scar was visible on the nape of his neck, amidst the close-cropped hair. The heavy fabric of his uniform gave out a smell of disinfectant which reminded me of the piles of blankets in the laundry, laced with a scent of soap; his boots and belt smelled of recently applied polish. The waiters were handing round some warm drink which was very strong; I took a glass from every tray that came around, and it was not long before I was well and truly drunk, glowing with alcoholic warmth, which somewhat lifted my dark mood. In the crammed lobby, the show went on; the silence preceding each number became increasingly tense and grave; so still was the room that you could hear the trees on the Esplanadi rustling in the wind. The voices of the nurses rang out with a mellow softness which was quite unlike the martial tones that I was used to hearing; they rose beguilingly in harmonic scales, then dropped again in geometric spirals. Yet for some reason their songs seemed to inspire the audience with the patriotic fervour normally aroused by a military march. The final song left the soldiers around me positively incandescent, and they burst into applause where joy and fear mingled in equal measure. It was not one of the gentle popular tunes they had been singing previously, but a march which everybody knew. I myself had also heard it somewhere, I could not remember where. At the first notes, one soldier tossed his cap into the air, others turned to hug each other, shouting words I could not understand; then, to a man, they rose to their feet, took one another by the shoulder and added their own deep voices to those of the choir. It was then that I recognized the march: suddenly I remembered the night of the bonfires, the icy road and my unknown companions singing in the dark. Perhaps they were indeed the very same men: I had seen nothing of them but the glowing tips of their cigarettes in the chill darkness. Now I realized that the smells too were familiar: *koskenkorva*, tobacco, sweat. Although I did not know the words, I too began moving my lips in imitation of the man next to me; I too applauded and thrust myself forward into the crowd which had formed around the soldiers, some of whom were weeping. The nurses on the dais were visibly moved, and had fallen silent, to listen to the soldiers; they looked hot and tired, yet quite composed. They remained in their rows, hands clasped, feet neatly together. Once the soldiers had fallen silent and the applause had finally died down, the usual atmosphere returned. As people filed slowly out, pulling on their overcoats, the waiters replaced the chairs around the tables and pushed the armchairs back into place beside the windows. After exchanging handshakes and military salutes, the soldiers too picked up their greatcoats and left the room. I saw them climb on to a military lorry, its headlights lighting up the whole room as it executed a turn in front of the hotel. The soldiers in regimentals, and the ambassadors, disappeared into the waiting limousines and drove away. Seated at the tables in the back of the room, the journalists had resumed their usual prattle about military strategy; one or two were at the bar, finishing their beer. The usual little glasses for *koskenkorva* now reappeared, together with the ashtrays. Several nurses had stayed behind and were now sitting with a couple of officers at a table a little to one side, where tea and cakes were being served, rather than *koskenkorva*; they were talking quietly and gathering the crumbs up from the tablecloth.

I had sat down in the first free armchair to hand, beside the window, and I was staring out of it at the blinding snow. The sudden calm after those rousing songs came as an anticlimax: having been in a sense part of their group, having shared their emotion, I now felt more alone than ever. The Kämp's usual bustle was not enough to keep my persistent anxiety at bay. My eye fell on my journalist friend, standing among a group of colleagues: he was holding forth in a language I did not know, putting forward his views in no uncertain terms, while another voice was raised in contradiction. I had no desire to throw myself into the usual journalists' discussions, to pretend to understand sentences which remained impenetrable to me, doggedly to pursue each sound until I managed to dovetail it in beside another I already knew, and hence grasp its meaning. It seemed to me that I would never have the strength to do that again; I felt an irresistible desire to give myself up to silence and to solitude, to let the world make of me what it would, sending me to a painless death, like that of soldiers falling asleep in the snow. Folding up my jacket and placing it on my knee, I glimpsed the label with the words 'Sampo Karjalainen' and slipped my finger absently behind it. It was a small piece of fabric secured by four stitches of black cotton, as firm as the sutures of a wound: four stitches which were all that held my life in place. Perhaps it had been that military march which had sent my thoughts back to Trieste; those frightened soldiers, so like those with me on board the Tübingen, and those others in the woods. I had not forgotten Doctor Friari's words; ever since my arrival in Helsinki, his advice had served as my rule of thumb, and had stood me in good stead. At first, it had seemed to work: as he had suggested, I had devoted myself systematically, indeed pigheadedly, to studying the Finnish language, I had allowed myself to be convinced that Finland was my country, that its people were my people, that those sounds were those of my own language. In moments of desolation, when my thoughts were at their blackest, I had stayed curled up before that flicker of hope, and so I had been saved. On such few clear days as there were, together with the pastor, I had gone to the headland at Katajanokka to see the sunrise, imagining that one day I too would be born afresh. It was not hard to give myself over to that universal need, the longing to belong. But my new adoptive identity remained a sham.

Each day meant starting again from scratch. The moment my attention lapsed, the moment I allowed my mind to wander, all the good work would be undone. The words stayed with me, my knowledge of the language became stronger and more rooted, but any sense of truly belonging to that place would have vanished. I had a distinct suspicion that I was running headlong down the wrong road. In the innermost recesses of my unconscious I was plagued by the feeling that, within my brain, another brain was beating, buried alive. The thought occurred to me that perhaps my sense of being permanently on the alert, my failure to immerse myself blindly in my new life, might stem from one single but serious omission. There was just one piece of Doctor Friari's advice that I had failed to follow: namely, to give myself over to the search for a lover. Somewhere within me a shell had formed, as hard as stone and equally impenetrable; I could feel it, under my skin, as though I could touch it. It was the kernel of my new being. To crack it open, to offer it to someone else, meant jeopardizing even that little I had managed to build up, meant that those sixteen letters of my name might be blown away, scattered to the four winds. I who did not yet know who I was, how could I forsake myself so soon? Who could be worthy of my trust?

So there I was, lost in painful thought, hunched over my bundle of blue cloth, staring pointlessly into the distance, when a familiar figure took shape at the watery margins of my vision. I recognized its gait as it lingered on its right leg, body and neck thrust slightly forward, as though it were seeking permission to enter my thoughts. It was the nurse who had met me on my arrival at the hospital, the one who had introduced me to Koskela and whom I had never seen since.

'Good evening! So it is you? From a distance, I wasn't sure,' she said, coming nervously forwards and making an effort at a smile.

'Good evening!' I answered, getting to my feet. I didn't know whether to shake her hand, and she didn't know whether or not to offer it. We ended up by exchanging something approaching a bow. My head was spinning, indeed I was probably reeling from too much alcohol; she must have noticed, and responded with a mixture of composure and embarrassment.

'Where have you been all this time?' I asked awkwardly.

'We nurses were mobilized, sent off to Mikkeli. We were supposed to have been going somewhere else, but we couldn't leave because of the bombing. Now we are off to Viipuri – tomorrow morning, in a troop train, to organize the refugee centre there, and … Oh, I'm sorry … how stupid I am! I wasn't thinking … I was forgetting …' When she spoke again it was more slowly, pronouncing each letter of each word with the utmost clarity:

'Mikkeli is a city – a big city – and, well, that's where we were, but …'

She was using her hands to give an idea of the city of Mikkeli. I broke in, smiling:

'Don't worry, my Finnish is much better now. I don't speak it well, in fact I speak it extremely badly, but I understand much more.'

She nodded in surprise.

'Oh, but you're right, congratulations! I wasn't paying attention! You've even got a slight Helsinki accent!' She was pressing her small hands together, desperately thinking of something to say.

'How about you? Still in the visitors' quarters?' Traces of red from her earlier embarrassment still lingered on her cheeks; as she spoke, she tried to thrust an unruly tuft of hair back under the cap from which it had broken loose, falling over her eyes.

'Yes, I'm still there. Bed number six, by the window!' I answered, a false note creeping into my voice. In my mind's eye I saw the six white beds on the red-tiled floor like six snow-covered tombstones.

She gave me an apologetic look, as though she felt personally responsible for my fate. Her green eyes had darkened slightly, as did her voice when she asked me:

'Is Doctor Lahtinen back yet?'

Within one question, I sensed another.

'No. Now they say he is in Petsamo,' I said, without much conviction.

'Perhaps he can't make it back. Travel is a problem, what with all the bombing …' she offered by way of explanation, though she herself did not seem to believe her own words.

'That's right. Perhaps he never will!' I shot back with a bitter smile. But I wanted to talk of other things; or perhaps I did not want to talk at all. I was forcing myself to be sociable, and it was taking its toll. I would have liked to find a quick way out of the entanglement, but some strange compulsion led me to carry on.

'Why don't we sit down?" I suggesting, pointing towards a table.

'That would be nice,' she replied, but she sounded

indifferent, nor did she make a move. She had blushed again and was looking down at her shoes, hoping I would not notice. I felt that she was regretting ever having acknowledged me.

She was a very slight girl, and fragile-looking, unlike most of the other nurses, who looked and moved like sturdy farmers' wives. She slipped off her cap and folded it up on her knee, running one hand quickly through her hair. The shifting colour of her eyes meant that there also seemed to be something changeable about her face: one moment she looked like a shy girl, whom I could scarcely imagine dealing with bomb-torn flesh, the next she looked like a grown woman, inured to the sight of suffering. Outside, the wind had died down and the snowflakes were drifting lightly towards the windows, settling into the spidery network of ice etched on to the panes; given a sense of warmth by the yellow glow of the candles, their white veiling offered a sense of security which was hard to resist.

'What lovely voices!' I said, nodding in the direction of her fellow-singers.

'Thank you! You're very kind. But then we're singing such lovely music!' she answered. I noticed that she was looking around uneasily, in search of some safe spot to rest her gaze. When they met mine, her eyes veered nervously away, like those of some startled creature. I too was peering around me, wondering how I might put her at her ease. Because, by now, I wanted her to stay; I would have liked to drive off her discomfiture with my bare hands.

'It is so good to sing: your lungs fill up with air, your blood runs faster, even your brain works better. That is how sad music becomes joyful music,' I said lumberingly, tripping over every word. But I was not sure that she had understood, because I often get mixed up between *surullinen* and *iloinen*' – sad and joyful.

'Singing is the most natural form of music; and the oldest!' she said distantly. I thought back to my lonely nights in Trieste, when I would repeat verses from songs I'd heard in the bars, quite without understanding them – just to have some words, any words, going through my head, anything to stave off the exhausting coming and going of my thoughts. Now I had a potential associate, someone to get to know, a friendship to nurture. But shaking off the crusty embrace of solitude entailed an effort.

'Do you sing?' she asked, taking heart.

'Yes, but only as children do, to pluck up courage when I am afraid.'

'And when are you afraid?'

'Often. Above all when I am alone, when there is too much silence. I'm always afraid that it will last forever.'

My words made her smile; clearly, they struck a chord. So as to have something to do with her hands, she had begun fiddling with one corner of her cap, rolling it up and watching it unroll.

'Silence is music too. At school, our singing teacher used to say that silence in music is like white in a water-colour; it's not a colour, but you need it in a painting. Silence is what is left around the patches of colour, and every painting ... '

I kept my eyes on her, but I was not seeing her. My thoughts were chasing one another pointlessly, never catching one another up. Her voice trailed away, and she looked at me doubtfully, ill-at-ease again.

'Perhaps what I am saying is too complicated? I'm sorry ... You express yourself so well, I quite forget ...'

'No, no,' I broke in, 'don't worry, I understand. Not everything, but enough. And when I don't understand, I myself make up what I want to hear!'

Then she laughed, and the sound was like a match struck in the dark room of my memory. I had the feeling I was remembering an identical laugh; but it was only a feeling.

'I like the image your singing teacher used,' I went on. 'Who knows, perhaps we could play pictures like symphonies, only we just don't know it!'

'You use words nicely, too,' she said. 'Now that you know it better, what is it that you most like about our language?'

'What do I like about it most?'

'Yes. A word, a phrase …'

'Well, I know this may strike you as strange, but what I like is the abessive!' I answered hesitantly.

'The abessive? But that's a case, a declension!' she shot back in amusement.

'Yes, a declension for things we haven't got: *koskenkorvatta*, *toivatta*, no *koskenkorva*, no hope, both are declined in the abessive. It's beautiful, it's like poetry! And also very useful, because there are more things we haven't got than that we have. All the best words in this world should be declined in the abessive!'

She burst out laughing, holding one hand in front of her mouth; but it was no good, because her amusement had spread to her eyes. I savoured the success of my witticism, felt a pleasant sense of warmth stealing over me.

I glanced out of the window. The journalists who were not staying in the Kämp were beginning to take their leave; I watched them setting off over the snow, shrouded in the white mist of their own breath, talking loudly and swinging their arms in order to keep warm. At that hour I too would usually be returning to the hospital: to my cold and empty room.

'What's the matter?' she asked in alarm, noting my sudden change of mood.

'Nothing, nothing,' I reassured her, shaking my head. 'We were talking about music!'

She looked relieved.

'Oh yes, music. What sort of music do you like most?'

'Well, I'm no expert – I don't go for anything difficult. Of the songs that you have just sung, I liked the last one very much.'

'The *Porilaisten marssi? Pojat kansan urhokkaan?* But that's a military march!'

'That's as may be. Anyway, the audience enjoyed it – it's cheerful.'

'The music maybe, but not the words!' She was amused, and was still rolling her cap up into ever larger curls.

'What are they about?'

'About the homeland, about blood and those who are prepared to die,' she explained gravely.

'Will you teach it me?'

'Well, there are more cheerful ones!' she protested.

'But that's the one I want!' I insisted. 'If you speak slowly, I could copy out the words.' I pointed to the notebook in my pocket, adding: 'I'll learn it by heart and then I'll be able to sing it when there's too much silence.'

She smiled; now I even saw a touch of tenderness in her eyes. She let her cap fall on her knee and placed her outspread hands upon the table; she clearly bit her nails.

'Just as you like!' she said, nodding in assent and looking around her, as though to check that no one was looking.

'I don't even know your name,' I said, opening up my notebook.

'Ilma,' she said in a low voice. 'It means air,' she added.

'Air?' I repeated, amused.

'Yes, like what you breath; or indeed what the weather is

like.' Once again she clenched her hands, so as to hide her fingers.

'So when the weather is bad, could you say that today it's bad Ilma?'

Clearly, no one had ever put it quite like that before.

'Why not?' she said, in some surprise. 'But, above all, the name Ilma means freedom. Because it lets you free to be what you are, to go where you want: free as air. That's what my father used to tell me. People called Eeva or Helena or Noora share their name with lots of others, so there's something stale about it; but Ilma is always new, always pure.'

The meaning of this last sentence escaped me. I had watched it emerging from her mouth, followed the sound of it for a time. Then, without my realising, my eyes had ventured in the direction of her own. I felt the muscles of my face relax: everything in me was now letting go.

I copied out the words of the *Porilaisten marssi*, barely understanding them, as though they were the ingredients of some secret spell, and now they struck me as more magical than ever. Of all the words I'd written in that notebook, it was the ones which had made the soldiers cry that most intrigued me. That they had to do with war was plain as a pikestaff. Some of them were quite long, full of repeated vowels, with umlauts like helmets and aitches like slung arms. Others, much shorter, chopped off by apostrophes, seemed to be waving their stumps in the direction of the empty line. Certain capital letters referred to places where famous battles had taken place, although I could not recognize them. I saw the word for flag, and it did indeed seem to flutter, making a snapping sound as it left one's lips.

'Now you must sing it!' suggested Ilma, suddenly warming

to her task, elbows on the table, hands awkwardly intertwined.

'I would like you to sing it with me,' I said, overcome with shyness.

'In march time, and till dawn?' she asked, suddenly playful.

'Till dawn!' I answered, getting up and pulling on my jacket. Drunk with an exhilaration I had never known, I let the words slip from my mouth careless of where they might lead me, although I sensed it might be far.

Ilma's face had lit up. The delicate sprinkling of freckles on her cheeks and cheekbones looked sharper, warmer, her expression suddenly unguarded, and a strange sense of reserve caused me to look away. I realized, then and there, that something was happening which I did not want to happen.

'Wait for me outside,' she said, pushing back her chair. Looking back through the ice-clad window pane I saw her rejoin her fellow-singers at the table, where her outline merged with the rest. There on the silent street the biting cold brought me to my senses: I felt unreasonably bothered, I wanted to run, to disappear back into my solitude, which now seemed both troublesome and comfortable, like some non-life-threatening disease. Now the very thought of even the most tenuous link between myself and that young woman filled me with dismay. How could I have yielded to such easy temptation? It must have been the alcohol. I was suddenly sickened by the idea of that unknown presence beside me, demanding warmth and care. I would be required to take an interest in another life and all its petty doings, to feign concern for a person who was nothing to me, to share my anxieties with someone else and agree to lower my gaze to meet their own. Above all I would have to listen – listen to someone else's story, sympathize, mull over their feelings, be dragged into sufferings not my own, though I would have to serve as comforter; have that face before me each day, pleading for understanding, pity, help; promising me joys I do not seek, affection I do not want to give. See my time merge, my boredom fuse, with hers; smell her smell on my clothes, pick out her shape along the street; sleep in her bed and wake up each morning, always the first, alone in the grey light, waiting for another endless day to start – to be spent with her, to be dragged out of silence by force and carried in my heart till evening, until the moment when darkness would return to drown out our solitude, both mine and hers. The idea was abhorrent to me. I was repelled by the way all those around me clung so doggedly to life, the way they were born again beneath the ruins, instantly rebuilding what the bombs had flattened, in the grip of that unquenchable desire to be brought back to life which is the scourge of the human race. My own instinctive desire was to get through such life as remained to me without sullying myself, with the least possible damage and the least involvement. Because mine was no longer a life, but a leftover, some leavings I had picked up along the way. To rediscover my true past was an impossibility; to seek out a future, a huge effort. Doctor Friari was right: language is our mother, and it is through language that we come into this world. But I had lost both, forever; to me, rebirth was denied. The best that I could do was to live out the remainder of the life I had as one smokes the last bit of a cigarette, in a hurry to get it over, already looking around for somewhere to throw the butt-end. Determined to avoid forging that dangerous link, I was about to walk off towards the darkness of the Esplanadi, but Ilma was already beside me; she placed her arm on my blue jacket, and I instinctively took it.

It was no longer snowing. The wind blowing in from the sea was now less cold. It smelled of seaweed, but also of resin: as though, on its journey from the open sea, before reaching the city it had become lost in the woods, soaking up the smell of the earth. The Esplanadi was deep in snow, its course marked only by two rows of bare trees.

When we reached the Mannerheimintie, it was dark and deserted; the great dark shapes of the buildings loomed above it, many with their windows still glued with strips of protective tape. We passed a group of soldiers, but fortunately they immediately turned off into the Aleksanterinkatu; perhaps they had just come out of the Capitol. They were talking loudly and walking at a fair pace, and we were irritated by the racket. But soon they were out of hearing, and we were plunged once more into the silence of the great avenue, streaked with tyre marks on the dirty snow. We turned into the Bulevardi and walked towards the sea. Ilma was walking in silence, but I thought I could catch the drift of her thoughts; she was working out what she was going to say. I looked at the sky, above the tangle of bare branches: it had a strange glow to it. Somewhere up there a wind must have been blowing; the odd gust made its way down among the trees, dislodging the snow from the branches. I could see the clouds fraying and whitening in the pale light of stars too distant to have any resonance.

'Now we can sing!' said Ilma in a whisper.

It was too dark to see her face, and I felt nothing but relief that she could not see mine. We walked faster as we sang, picking our way between heaps of snow-covered rubble, along the dismal road suddenly enlivened by our song. The city lay around us, motionless, crouched like a hunted animal. Disembodied and brazen, our voices were dashed against the walls, falling back upon us in fragments. What with the singing and the marching, I was soon out of breath; but the more I sang, the emptier my head became. At the end of each verse Ilma would remind me of the words of the next. I followed her as best I could, and I felt as though I were marching towards the front, towards the Russian batteries hidden beyond the horizon; or towards that battlefield which I myself had become. Hearing me flounder over some difficult word Ilma would laugh, tightening her grip upon my arm, and it was by that arm that I felt clamped to the life I had decided to clutch at; that life I had so often seen flowing at my feet without finding the courage to leap into it, to wallow in it, like the rest. Now I was allowing myself to be dragged along, into song and down that street, away from loneliness, away from silence; away from myself.

When we reached the shores of Hietalahti Bay, we came to a stop; it was so quiet that you could hear the fat raindrops falling from the trees; and I too was a raindrop, I too was a tree. I was the snow, and I was no longer frightened of melting, of running down the streamlets into the sea, to merge with the relentless march of all that is endlessly transformed and never dies. For the first time I had found the courage to leap out of my beleaguered consciousness and mingle with something different from myself. I had gone down into the slime of life, my feet experiencing its disagreeable consistency. My awareness of this careless intermingling made me at once euphoric and dismayed: I had become vulnerable. My fragile memory, hothouse-reared, kid-glove tended, now lacked all protection; now parasites and mould could attack and destroy all that had cost me so dear to nurture. Now that I was alive, I might also die. A door had opened up before me, and it filled me with foreboding: to go through it meant steeping myself in life, letting each cell merge with millions of others, becoming part of that chaotic brew of organisms which is life, where the individual is insignificant and life and death are mere moments, ways through towards some other place, some point in the universe where everything is rushing headlong – to disappear. On the one hand I was drunk on that new sensation of surrender and belonging, on the other I was alarmed by the idea of losing control of my individuality. I regretted that I would never be able to go back to that freezing evening when I had gone into the Kämp and sat down among those soldiers with their unknown uniforms.

'It's starting to thaw,' said Ilma, pausing to listen. She looked around, narrowed her eyes and added: 'Can you hear, the wind has changed? It's coming from the sea.'

We both looked behind us at the dark mass of the city, then turned towards the white expanse of sea.

'Does that mean there will be no more snow?' I asked.

'It will rain. A lot. Everything will turn to mud.'

'But the trees will come into leaf.'

'That takes time. Here, spring is the worst season. The earth and sky soak up the mud churned up by all the rain; even the seagulls get spattered with it when they come to peck at rubbish in the puddles. Everything that has died in winter goes bad only in spring, because the ice keeps it alive for months. You'll see, there will be a smell of rotten wood, dead animals and stagnant water, all coming from the woods. It's like that on battlefields: it's only now that many mothers will weep; only now will the earth be soft enough for digging graves. That is another thing the summer does: it frees us from the dead.'

In front of us the ice was creaking, the trees were dripping and the clouds breaking up in the darkness of the sky, swept by a gale that we down here could hardly hear. Ilma fell silent, let go of my arm and turned towards the open sea. Now I could smell her hair: it smelled of smoke and lacquer; it smelled of life. I felt an urge to take her by the shoulders, to take her in my arms, to hold that being made as I was made. But something held me back: each of us was locked into an equal solitude, lonely conditions which touched one another but did not blend, like two drops of different liquids. We carried on walking around the bay, towards the hill in Kaivopuisto Park; a shapeless bit of moon had emerged from a strip of cloud piled up on the horizon, its glancing light gashing the countryside like machine-gun fire. Shadows dense as pitch danced down from the trees on to the walls of the buildings, carving dark, unsettling fissures in the snow. The houses thinned out as we approached the hill; Ilma was walking a few steps ahead of me, as though she were in a hurry to reach her goal.

'I want to show you a secret,' she said.

She walked quickly up the slope, turning around every now and again. I could hear her breath, and the splashing sound our steps made in the wet snow; from time to time the wind would send a lock of our hair flying over our faces like a long scratch. I was having trouble keeping up with her, and would stop every so often to draw breath. I sensed, from her enthusiasm and her determined step, that she had something specific in mind. She stopped in the middle of a field of untouched snow, on the brow of a downward slope running towards a little cobbled lane.

'Here we are!' she exclaimed breathlessly, pointing towards a great tree, gnarled and bare, which forked into two almost at its base, one branch running immediately upwards, the other running horizontal to the ground for several feet before doing the same, so as to form a seat. Ilma went to sit on it, brushing the remains of the snow from its smooth bark, and casting a shadow which looked alarmingly like that of some prehistoric animal.

'This is the magic tree – the tree of happy memories! It's here that I hang all the good things that have happened to me in this city. Of course, it's more impressive when it's in leaf – summer evenings are the time to come here, when the light is red and the air taut as a sail. That's when it casts its spell. Would you like me to tell you how it works?'

I nodded, and went to sit beside her on the seat.

'Whenever I meet someone I get on well with, I bring them here, talk to them here, let the tree take in something of our memories, and the magic starts to work. Then each time I come here that memory will return: that moment, that person are mine for ever, here, inside the magic tree!'

'Do you have memory trees everywhere you go?'

'No, only here.'

'Why only here?'

'Because in this life you have a right to just one memory tree. Otherwise, it would be too easy, people would just rush from one tree to the next so that nothing would ever be forgotten, so that nothing of one's own memories would be left lying around. Then nothing would be forgotten, and memories would cease to exist.'

'But without memories there would be no nostalgia, either,' I objected.

'That's true. So how would people carry on living? After all, we live in hope that a memory will come back – that it will prove to be a premonition.'

A prolonged silence followed. I listened to the wind as it whistled through the branches; I wished that they could speak instead of me, for I had nothing more to say. But rather than keeping silent, I persisted:

'And why would you want to remember me?'

It gave me a certain painful pleasure to say these words;

nor did I try to soften their meaning with my tone of voice. Amidst the throng of rowdy thoughts that had surged through my mind during that night, I recognized the face of my own solitude: it was my damnation and my raison d'être. It was calling me now; I had to go. Ilma bowed her head; she knew what I was thinking.

'So that this night may be remembered, so that it won't fall into the dark pit of everything that's past,' she answered bitterly.

'So you hope that this night will come back? That it will be a premonition of something else?'

My question was badly formulated, put together in haste without the words being properly sewn together. Ilma had to think for a moment before she understood what I meant.

'I don't know yet. I haven't got the heart to hope for anything. I'm making do with storing up things to hope for! Time will tell me which to continue hoping for and which to set aside,' she replied at last, still forcing her mouth into a smile, but it was a ghost of what had gone before.

I didn't understand her answer, but I didn't ask for explanations; they no longer held any interest for me. Ilma was silent for a moment; she was breathing hard, perhaps holding back tears.

'Don't you have any hopes at all? Is there nothing that you wish for?' she managed to ask again, though she was clearly having difficulty getting the words out.

'Yes, there is: I hope to find some memory of me in someone else; I hope to find someone who can tell me about even one single day in my past life: about one summer's afternoon when I was a child, some outing, what games I played. Because surely I too must have run around a courtyard kicking a ball?'

I had spoken emphatically, almost angrily; but my tirade

vanished into the unresponsive darkness as though I had not spoken.

'But perhaps I'm wrong,' I went on bitterly. 'Perhaps that's not what I should be looking for.'

'Tomorrow this will already be a memory, a small seed pearl,' said Ilma after a long sigh. I was rejecting her and still she was trying to comfort me.

'To keep a memory, you have to have somewhere to store it,' I shot back tersely.

'You can glue it into your album of memories along with the *Porilaisten marssi*. Night with Ilma, you could call it.'

Her forced smile irritated me.

'I have no memory, I have no past. My souvenir album ends practically before it has begun,' I protested.

'Who cares about the beginning of a fairy story? It's hearing the end that keeps children awake till all hours, with the book hidden under the covers, curled up in the candlelight, shivering with fear at the weird noises all houses make at night.'

A falsely cheerful note had crept into her voice; it rang out firmly, then trailed off suddenly into silence. She had responded to my every remark with the most persuasive words that she could muster, whereas I had flung the most cruel that I could marshal back in her face. With her silence, she seemed to be asking me why. Then we both stopped talking: nothing, we felt, could fill the gap that had opened up between us, however small: we would bear it within us always, until the end of time. Because of those few fateful moments, our feelings would never weigh equally upon the scales: there would always be something left over, some unspendable small change. I had sought her affections, I had let her run towards me, then I had rejected her. For no reason: just for the subtle pleasure of disappointing her and proving to myself that any attempt at breaking out of my solitude was vain. I was enjoying my suffering: by fooling myself that I was fighting it, I was putting it to some purpose. My lost memory had become my excuse for giving up on life. Now, in the moonlight, each could have seen the other's face; but both of us were looking straight ahead. As in the bay below us, ice had had once more closed in upon me.

'I'll write to you when I'm in Viipuri,' said Ilma, almost as though to reassure herself she could still speak.

'And what will you write about?'

'Memories,' she said, laughing loudly now, as though by way of reproach.

'Do you at least promise that you'll answer?'

'I promise,' I said, barely audibly.

Now we were back on the Mannerheimintie, plodding along side by side in silence, heads bowed. A distant strip of grey above the sea marked the start of a hard-won dawn: soon light would trickle from the close mesh of the sky, casting its faint glow over what was left of the snow, over the muddied earth. In the open space below us, black motorized columns were crawling over the snow like snakes, breaking up and reforming, breathing out steam. A hoarse whistle broke the silence; the lights of the station were coming closer, there was the sound of the odd engine in the distance. Suddenly Ilma took my arm again and broke into the *Porilaisten marssi*, but her voice was thick with emotion and I had trouble making out the words. I tried to join in, to keep her company, to cover her voice with my own, but my head was heavy and I found that the words were suddenly beyond me. Outside the main Post Office, an elderly man on the other side of the road stopped in his tracks to look at us. He was well-dressed, and wearing a fur hat; he took off his gloves, hooked his walking-stick over his arm and started to clap. The walls of the Post Office building sent his solitary applause echoing back to us; amplified by the silence and filling the square with that martial sadness that bodes defeat, it stayed with us as we walked under the lanterns clasped in the bronze hands of the colossal statues on the station façade. The troop train for Viipuri was already on the platform. The whole place was in ferment: soldiers in brand new uniforms and gleaming helmets were boarding by the dozen, amidst much stamping of feet; groups of nurses gathered around their luggage were seeking each other out and gesturing to one another. A loudspeaker was barking out names and destinations. I said goodbye to Ilma before she got on to the train: I could not bear the idea of seeing her leaning out of the window. Amidst all that bustle I quickly pulled off my gloves, took her hand and squeezed it hard, then fled, without another glance.

The *Porilaisten marssi* is indeed a song that speaks of war and banners fluttering over battlefields; I hummed it again to myself, alone this time, looking out over the frozen bay, in the snow-covered Kaivopuisto Park, standing motionless next to the tree of memories. I sang it loudly under the cold covers until alcohol and exhaustion won out in the fight against anxiety.

Here the manuscript is strangely blank, with just the odd disjointed phrase, Ilma Kovisto's address in Viipuri and the text of the Porilaisten marssi. *I felt that it should be included here, not just for documentary completeness, but because of what it also means for me: exile, the absurdity of war and all its menacing allure, personal defeat. Glued on to the back of this page I also found the programme of the benefit-*

concert given on 24 March 1944 by the choir of the Lotta-Svärd at the hotel Kämp. Apart from the Porilaisten marssi it also included the following pieces: Oi kallis Suomenmaa, Jääkärimarssi, Isänmaalle, Suomalainen rukous, Laps' Suomen, Siniristilippumme, Terve Suomeni maa, Vala and Olet maamme armahin Suomenmaa. The pianist in the over-large uniform was Sergeant Veijo Vihanta, from the corps of frontier guards. The unknown soldiers belonged to the native Karelian Brigade, which was decimated on Lake Ladoga in June 1944.

After reading these pages I too went to the tree of happy memories; and I too found my own. In summer I used to go to play near it as a child, in the copse next to the Observatory. After school my mother and a woman friend would take me to the park and sit there chatting, while I would set about playing with a vengeance. On the esplanade behind the port I would create a world of my own, full of adventure, hiding behind the hedges and secretly observing the park keeper as he sat on a bench eating his lunchtime herring. He would take off his hat with its shiny leather brim – how I envied him that hat – and set the table with his thermos of coffee, a packet of herrings and a screw of paper containing berries. I was a bloodthirsty Viking who had recently landed on those shores in order to put the city to the sword. I would take the park keeper prisoner and drag him in chains to the president's residence, like the slaves of Sigtuna in the coloured illustrations in my reading-book. Then I would rush off to sink the enemy ships as they rode at anchor in the port. But no sooner had I gone down the hill again than I would come face to face with my mother, who would grab me firmly by the arm, complaining that she had been calling for me for quite some time. My love affairs, on the other hand, would be conducted elsewhere, in the streets

*behind the harbour at Pohjoissatama, between Kruununhaka
and Tervasaari, where I would hide in doorways, never weary
of clasping a body which, by virtue of repeated embrace, I
deluded myself that I might cause to enter mine. But I didn't go
down there: I want the memory I still have of those places to
remain intact, softened by time, cleansed of all pain. Perhaps,
indeed, the day will come when memory will ebb away from
those images too, letting them fade into oblivion. Here I
agree with Miss Koivisto: never to forget anything would be
unbearable.*

    Porilaisten marssi

    *Pojat, kansan urhokkaan,
    Mi Luolan, Lützin, Leipzingin
    Ja Narvan mailla vertaan vuoti,
    Viel'on Suomi voimissaan,
    Voi vainolaisen hurmehella peittää maan.*

    *Pois, pois, rauhan toimi jää,
    Jo tulta kohta kalpa lyö
    Ja vinkuen taas lentää luoti.
    Joukkoon kaikki yhtykää,
    meit'entisajan sankarhenget tervehtää.*

    *Kauniina väikkyy muisto urhojemme,
    Kuolossa mekin vasta kalpenemme.
    Eespäin rohkeasti vaan,
    Ei kunniaansa myö
    Sun poikas milloinkaan!*

    Uljaana taistolippu liehu,

Voitosta voittohon
Sä vielä meitä viet!
Eespäin nyt kaikki, taisto alkakaa,
Saa sankareita vielä nähdä Suomenmaa!

Although we had a relationship of mutual trust, the pastor had never asked me about my accident in as many words; he had never made any reference to my short past, but I knew he was aware of it – he had read Doctor Friari's letter, which was kept in the archives in the reception area, in the grey folder, still without a name. In his dealings with me, Koskela always tried to act with the utmost naturalness. But he could never treat me quite like one of his own: my story was too mystifying, my condition too anomalous. So he ended up by treating me as a sort of student of his language for whom he had been called upon to devise an intensive course in quintessential Finnishness. With teacherly resolve, he tried to focus my attention on the simple things of everyday life; he tried to show me that the mundane here-and-now – that area where my humdrum mind was floundering – was indeed all man can truly know. But he himself was unconvinced of what he was preaching, because he too had a present without a future. The pastor lived every day as though it were an act of obligatory unpaid labour – as though it were his last, as though everything had to be set out in perfect order prior to death. His true aim, in all likelihood, was to nudge me towards a place where I would be able to survive on my own; to edge me out of that dull despair which is the prelude to madness. But his instinctive cynicism showed through at every turn. That avoidance of regret, which he imposed upon me like some spiritual exercise, together with his blind conviction that each day would be the last, turned my existence into a mad rush towards nothingness.

Each hour spent with the pastor was so intense, so thought-provoking, that there was no room for dread. In that portion of my thoughts that I had put in the pastor's care, no doubts could grow: nothing grew there. Without realizing it, I was marching beside him, escorting him to his own end.

That day, he had come to sit beside me in the refectory. I had never seen him eat there before; I assumed he ate his meals at the table in the sacristy. Without a word, he began drinking his soup with his usual systematic haste. When he had wiped the bowl clean and devoured the last bit of bread, he pushed the tin tray away from him and raised his eyes.

'The ice is melting! The Germans have reached Uhtua!' he pronounced cautiously, as though imparting a secret.

'Soon it will be up to us again,' he added darkly. 'And then we will have to do what the great *runoilija* Väinämöinen did: find the right words to break the spell. Because in essence the war we're fighting now is the same war we Finns have been engaged in ever since our birth, the one we started so long ago with Pohjola, queen of the shades: to speak, and sing, more loudly than the rest. You who are studying our language, you must know this. To sing is *lauluaa*, which also means to enchant. But for the ancient Finnish poets, to sing – or, if you like, to chant – and to enchant, were one and the same. Anyone who could sing could also enchant. Not for nothing does the *Kalevala* begin with a singing contest between two singers, or *runoilija*. Joukahainen, presumptuous and ill-prepared, dares to challenge the ageing Väinämöinen in the art of magic song and is beaten by him, silenced by his art. Väinämöinen puts stone shoes on Joukahainen's feet, wooden breeches on his legs, a heavy weight upon his chest, piles of stones upon his shoulders, stone gloves on his hands, a granite cape upon his head. This is what the *Kalevala* says. Such is the magic of song. But only those who are fully acquainted with the power of the word should dare to have recourse to its magic!'

Now the refectory was emptying out. Weak rays of sun were filtering through its high windows, casting a gentle light over the violet smoke rising from the cigarettes of the last few stragglers; clouds of dust swarmed in the gilded air. Some nurses had already started cleaning the floor, dragging heavy pails of steaming water behind them and dipping soapy cloths into them. From time to time, their metallic clang drowned out the pastor's words, causing him to raise his voice in irritation. When he was saying something complicated, he knew that he had to repeat himself, and break the more complex sentences into their simpler component parts so that I had a chance of understanding. But, in the grip of habit, with time he had come to use this method indiscriminately, each time he addressed me. That was how he proceeded that day in the refectory, heedless of the nurses as they looked in his direction, shooting him politely curious glances.

'Väinämöinen was above all a shaman, a worker of magic. Such shamans used to drug themselves on magic mushrooms, whose hiding places in the woods were known only to them. These mushrooms sent them into a state of ecstasy which cut them off from the real world: they would leave their own bodies to hover somewhere outside reality, where they would discover signs, receive revelations, cures for illnesses, formulae which would drive off wild beasts and serve as protection against injury. They were vouchsafed the world of visions, of another realm, of dreams. The greatest of all these shamans was the giant Antero Vipunen: he travelled so far from his own body that he could never get back into it. His words were so powerful that they changed the course of nature; even today, in his vain effort to return to it, his soul wanders around the tangle of brambles that his abandoned body became. And it is to Antero Vipunen that Väinämöinen goes to ask for the three words he was lacking to complete his magic boat, the one that was to take him to the land of Pohjola. In the primitive world everything was new and boundless, even pain. That is why, when they are feeling pain, the heroes of the *Kalevala* can split the eternal ice with a single blow of the foot, raze a forest to the ground with a single sabre cut, bring about a migration of cranes with a single shout. That is why, even today, we Finns are capable of infinite endurance. Soon the Russians will attack, and then it will take all the strength we can muster, all our powers of endurance, all the words of Antero Vipunen to stop them. Nothing good has ever come out of the East: only invasions. Relentless waves of Slavs have poured repeatedly over our land; war against them will cease only when we have exterminated them or driven them off. Because, by some quirk of fate, we have stuck ourselves right in their path. If only the Turks had stopped at Samarkand!' he exclaimed, waving his arms in the air with rage.

The nurses' mops were already lapping at our feet; the floor was steaming from the boiling water. The smell of ammonia had won out against that of turnip soup. My thoughts were with the giant Antero Vipunen, locked out of his own body, and I knew how he felt. I had not understood the story of the magic boat, but it was too complicated to ask, so I decided to ask what the word *kattohaikarat* meant instead. Koskela rose suddenly to his feet, imitating a large bird with a long beak and outspread wings. The nurses looked at him wryly.

'No lessons today; I'm expecting visitors,' he said abruptly, and his eyes, now strangely cloudy, were also strangely bright.

I took my jacket from the coat rack and followed him from a distance into the corridor, then into the courtyard. As usual, I had not slept much that night, and was thinking of going to lie down in the visitors' quarters, but then I saw him heading for the church, and automatically went after him, reaching the sacristy door just in time to hear the key turn in the lock. That was the day that I learned that Olof Koskela took drugs. I saw him through the sacristy window. Seated at the empty table, he was slipping a pinch of some greenish powder under his tongue; it looked a bit like mildew, and he had taken it out of a small pocket snuff-box. Then he placed his elbows firmly on the table, stretched his fingers out over the veining in the wood, so similar to that on his own hands, and stayed there motionless, staring interminably at the wall in front of him, as though he could see something there: something infinitely small, or the size of the wall itself, I do not know, but it was as though it could be seen only from that particular spot. As it appeared, his features changed, his face became a mask, with empty eye sockets and a gaping mouth. The being seated in that sparsely furnished room was no longer a man: he was a totem, with a tough wooden skin. On making this discovery, at first I felt betrayed: I felt that even the pastor was deserting me. His strength of spirit, which had brought me such support and comfort, appeared to me now merely as some chemically-produced elation, on a par with my own *koskenkorva*-fuelled drunkenness. But this feeling was short-lived. I preferred to believe that, like Antero Vipunen, the pastor was going down into his unconscious in search of the right word, the answer to all pain. Finding him suddenly so vulnerable, I felt that he was closer to me. I realized that his harsh exterior served not to shut others out, but to shut himself in: to contain the unstable magma which seethed within him. The order he imposed upon his days was a form of self punishment, meted out as penance for the unruly ramblings of his spirit; the rigour with which he went about his daily round offered some protection against the irrational into which he periodically ventured. Now I found his various fixations more understandable: behind his dogged insistence that the missals be tidily stacked away each night, the candlestick cleaned, the pencils sharpened and the brass numbers indicating the psalms put back where they belonged – behind all this lay the fear of the obscure forces he unleashed within himself. Perhaps, I thought, it was even possible that all that trawling through narcotic worlds might have caused him to stumble upon some trace of my own past.

After Ilma's departure, my life resumed its dubious normality. I swallowed the days down whole, like shots of *koskenkorva*; I had also started to resume my regular visits to the Kämp, and my occupation as general dogsbody. At times I would accompany my journalist friend on his expeditions around the city and the outlying countryside, together with an eccentric ambassador friend of his, visiting bombed-out villages and abandoned prison camps. As Ilma had predicted, everything was now sunk in yellowish mud. The streets were slimy canals down which our vehicle slithered, sending up spurts of mushy filth. Nature was slow to reawaken; in the fields, the trees still looked completely dead, and the huts where the refugees were lodged added further desolation to the landscape. The fact that the days were drawing out seemed to be serving no purpose; for weeks on end the sky remained smoky and louring, so near the earth that it too looked as if it were soiled with mud. In the time for which I could find no other use, I wandered round the city, calling on all the people called Karjalainen I found in the phonebook. Mostly, no one came to the door; or I would be shown into dark hallways to find old women seated stock-still beside the window, or frightened families who looked at me with alarm, fearing bad news. I went up the stairs of half-empty buildings, repeated my name and received blank looks in return. I unearthed dusty little worlds of people living buried in their own houses, with nothing but a bed, a table and a tea chest of potatoes covered with a scrap of sacking. I would be met by limp bodies whose reptilian movements spoke of long confinement; by absent glances, muffled voices. They responded to my questions with incomprehensible answers, repeating them in precisely the same words when I shook my head to tell them I had not understood.

One afternoon at the end of April I ventured as far as the new parts of Vallila, where the houses petered out and the roads crossed the railway to disappear into the open country. The day was mild and windy, the sky streaked with white. It had not rained for several days and the wind had at last dried out the ever-present layer of mud. The tracks of dried earth running across the fields looked like petrified snakes, with the odd military lorry lumbering along them, sending up a line of dust like a whip-lash trail of dynamite, glowing on the horizon. I was walking along a road called Teollisuuskatu, looking for number 456, which turned out to be almost the last house, near the brick buildings by the railway. It was a large modern apartment block, with stone balconies and small windows, the main door separated from the road by a stretch of grass. I went into a gravelled courtyard, lined with rows of closed shutters. A red-haired man was mending a motorbike by one of the walls, his tools spread out beside him on a scrap of cloth; he was kneeling on the ground and peering into the open engine.

'Excuse me, I'm looking for the Karjalainens. Heikki Karjalainen,' I explained.

'Second floor,' he said, pointing towards a flight of stairs; I could hear my steps echoing out through the courtyard as I climbed them. Seeing a brown-painted door bearing a nameplate carved with the words H. Karjalainen, I stopped and listened. A smell of musty cellars rose through the air; somewhere, a wireless was playing. I pressed the brass bell; the door opened a crack and an elderly man appeared.

'Yes?'

'Are you Mister Karjalainen?'

'Yes.'

'I need to talk to you. Can I come in?'

The man peered at me from over his spectacles, hesitating for a moment before he let me in. I found myself in the gloom of a shabby living room. The only window looked out over the courtyard; I noticed a crumpled newspaper lying on a threadbare sofa. The wall opposite the window was occupied by a dark sideboard, on which stood a ticking wooden clock, decorated with stags.

'If it's to do with Sampo, we already know,' the old man whispered.

'Sampo?' I gave a start. It was only then that I noticed a shelf cluttered with sacred images in one corner of the room, lit by a little oil lamp, in whose flickering light I now glimpsed the black-edged portrait of a sailor in uniform. I took down the photograph and went up to the window. His jacket was identical to my own; or rather it had the same collar, but the buttons were metal rather than horn. The old man followed me, shuffling around the room.

'Second Lieutenant Manner has already been. He said it happened on the twenty-third of August.'

I stared at that face as though my life depended on it, seeking some resemblance to my own: eyes, mouth, hair. Could it be me?

'The twenty-third of August,' I repeated as if in a daze.

'Yes, the day my wife and I went to eat at Kappeli's to celebrate our wedding anniversary. I remember it well. We should never have done it, I could feel it that same evening as we were getting on to the bus. Something just wasn't right: that red sun on the sea, our long shadows on the cobbles in the square. When you have a son who's on active service, you don't go to a restaurant. We were eating baked salmon and rice pudding while our son was dying; and what place is there in this world for a mother and father who have lost their son?'

The old man left the question dangling in the charged silence of the room; he was looking towards the window, and the pale light from the courtyard was reflected in his thick spectacles; behind the lenses, his eye sockets looked like two reptiles in jars of formalin.

'That news drove Leena clean out of her mind,' he whispered, pointing towards the half-closed door of the next room. 'She's like one of those soldiers who've trodden on a mine and got off scot-free. You must have seen them: they just sit there like statues. They look perfectly all right, just like you and me; but they don't see, and they don't hear. They're like the walking dead.'

I looked around me in some disquiet, running my eyes over the room – the sideboard, the sofa, the marble table – in search of some familiar object.

'What ... what exactly happened to Sampo?' I asked.

'Second Lieutenant Manner said it all happened very fast. A torpedo. The Riilahti listed, caught fire and sank. All dead; but they never found Sampo.'

'Never found him?' I asked sharply. Noting my sudden agitation, he looked me straight in the eye for the first time.

'Did you know him? Was he a friend of yours?'

'I … I am called Sampo Karjalainen!' I burst out, clutching the sailor's portrait in both hands.

At that moment a shriek tore through the silence of the room: an old woman in a dressing-gown appeared at the door, walking towards us with staring eyes and shrieking 'Sampo! Sampo!' I retreated to the other side of the table in alarm.

'Leena! Calm down! Leena!' repeated the old man gently as he tried to restrain the woman; after a few moments she collapsed on to the sofa, fixing me with a frightened stare and whimpering.

'Leena! What's got into you? The gentleman won't do you any harm, he's just come to pay us a visit!' He turned back to me, pulling a chair out from the table.

'Please, do make yourself at home! What a fool I am, I haven't even asked you to sit down! We have so few visitors, you see, I'm out of practice. Now, let's make a pot of tea! Eh, Leena? A nice cup of tea for the gentleman! A cup of tea, that's what we need,' said the old man, opening the sideboard and setting teacups, saucers and teapot down haphazardly upon the table.

'Let's talk about Sampo,' he added, carrying on talking as he went into the little kitchen, where I could hear him striking a match.

'Sampo liked to have tea with us when he got back from work. Always cheerful, that boy! He would sit just where you're sitting now, and tell us all the latest news.'

Pinned to my seat, I couldn't take my eyes off the old woman; rocking from side to side, she stared straight back at me, repeating the fateful name under her breath. I could read it on her lips, as they opened and closed, soundlessly, non-stop.

'Then he would go and have a wash, get on his motorbike and go into town. He bought it with his savings, you know. A German machine, a fine piece of work! That was all he was interested in. Now we've sold it to a neighbour. What good is a motorbike to us?'

The old man now appeared holding a steaming teapot, which he put down on the table; the steam wafted through the room, and now there was suddenly a smell of old soup, of cigarettes forgotten on some painted surface.

'He worked as a lathe operator, did you know? And he'd found a good job – with Abloy, quite near here, the firm which makes locks.'

I picked up my teacup absently and put it down next to the photograph of Sampo Karjalainen which the old man had left lying on the table.

'But his real passion was for his motorbike; whenever he had a moment he would go down to polish it. On summer evenings he'd take it out to the stretch of grass in front of the building and stay there listening to the engine, looking at the smoke from the exhaust. Then he'd drive off into the blue yonder, and that was the last you'd see of him! Isn't that right, Leena?'

The old man had sat down on the sofa, next to his wife, holding her steaming teacup, stirring it slowly and helping the old woman to take sips from it, which she did from between half-closed lips; no sooner was her mouth free than she persisted with her endless muttering.

'Leena's taking tea with us, aren't you, Leena? Just like when Sampo was here, making us both laugh. And could he make us laugh, that Sampo! Telling us about his friends in the factory, those two brothers, do you remember?'

The clock on the sideboard ticked on quietly in the silences between his broken sentences; from the courtyard came the sound of an engine backfiring.

'Only Sampo could make that thing do what he wanted. Isn't that so, Leena?'

I suddenly felt sick: in need of light, fresh air.

'I really must be off!' I exclaimed, pushing the cup away, walking backwards towards the door and turning the handle.

The old man shuffled after me, but did not try to stop me leaving. He blinked behind his spectacles, staring at a gap in the balcony as he spoke.

'Sampo, please be careful with that motorbike. Don't drive too fast, and don't be back late; and don't drink too much, either, Sampo! It's dangerous!'

I left without bothering to close the door and rushed down the stairs. On the pavement outside, the red-haired man was doggedly kicking the start pedal of the motorbike; the engine would turn over for a moment, spark briefly into life and then become flooded. A ray of sunlight falling through the main door lit up the dust and violet smoke suspended in mid-air over the pit of the courtyard. I went out with relief into the airy street, into the wan evening sunlight and began to run; I did not stop until I had left the place well behind me, stopping at last amidst the ruins of a bombed-out factory, where I sat down on a low wall, closed my eyes and breathed deeply, until my head began to spin.

At the bottom of this page the address, Teollisuuskatu 456, the date, 23 August 1943, the name of Second Lieutenant Manner, and of the ship, the Riilahti, have been noted down in block capitals, with a line drawn round them. Next to the name of the ship the author had pencilled in the word 'minelayer', and a question mark.

At the Admiralty I was told that the minelayer Riilahti had been sunk by the Russians off Tiskeri on 23 August 1943; what remained of it, broken into two, had been located, and is currently lying at a depth of 70 metres. The twenty-four members of the crew all perished; their bodies had been recovered: all except for that of Seaman Sampo Karjalainen, which was still missing. The family had been given a commemorative medal.

The clerk at the Admiralty insisted on showing me a photo of the Riilahti, taken in the summer of 1940 during a naval review. The image of the ship moored at the quayside, with the Finnish flag flying and the sailors massed in the bow, reminded me of the Finnish merchantmen which used to arrive in the port of Hamburg. For me, each one was a piece of Finland. Their arrival had become a regular event, one which gradually came to punctuate the days in my calendar, the changes in season. In spring it was the Pyhä Henrik, which brought timber to Hamburg from Oulu and returned laden with machine tools; in summer it was the oil tanker Pietarsaari and in December the Petsamo, which supplied the ports of Kemi and Pori with grain. Not to mention all the others which called in at Hamburg en route to more distant places. Every evening I would mingle with the sailors when they gathered in the Finnish church, as though they were my family. I wanted to shake hands with each of them, and had to restrain myself from seeming too outgoing, for they themselves were reserved and solitary by nature. My heart lifted when I could render them some service: such simple medical assistance as I could offer made me feel that I was contributing to the well-being of my country, redeeming sins that I had not in fact committed and earning myself some possibility of return. Some ships had been plying the same route for years, and the captains knew me well: we had built up a relationship of mutual trust and respect. After a certain point, without my even having to ask, they would bring me bundles of newspapers. The crews who arrived during the Christmas period never failed to bring me some present or other: some bit of furniture or carpentry tool for the pastor, liquor and cigarettes for me which, although I did not smoke, I kept like so many precious relics. The captain of the Rosvo Roope, which shuttled between Helsinki and Hamburg every three months transporting iron ore, would unfailingly bring me the books I had asked for, together with some magazine or record for my mother. Hearing those Finnish voices in our Hamburg apartment lulled me into the cruel illusion that I was at home, but my mother seemed to be unaffected. She was half-German, but cultivated her Finnish side assiduously. With the help of those records and magazines she kept herself more or less up to date with the latest Finnish fads and fancies – only three months behind. I on the other hand was irritated by that artificial Finland; the music my mother would play incessantly on the gramophone aroused unwelcome memories in me. Yet, when I hear those tunes again today, it is the thought of her that wells up in my mind, and her 'apartment Finland' lives on again, as long as the song lasts, in empty rooms.

The Tree of Happy Memories

The letters which follow were copied into the notebook by the author himself. Although some parts are repeated several times, and others are underlined or quoted again elsewhere in the manuscript, it is to be presumed that, in one place or another, the letters appear here in their entirety. Despite having authorized me to publish them, Miss Ilma Koivisto, who wrote these letters, made it known that I should not reread the originals and asked to be allowed to keep them. I am respecting her request, and I thank her for her help in elucidating certain passages whose meaning was unclear to me, clarifying personal references and allusions which an outsider would not have been able to understand. I do not propose to dwell on Miss Koivisto's feelings, but I must say that I was moved by the evident passion and sincerity which her words convey. If the author of this document had abandoned his pointless search for his past, and yielded rather to the pleasures of the present, perhaps his fate would have been different. Sometimes human thought gets lost in the warren of its own logic, becomes a slave to a geometry which is an end in itself, whose aim is no longer the understanding of reality, but the bolstering of some prior assumption. We are such monstrous egoists that we would rather destroy ourselves pursuing false truths than admit that we are on the wrong track. To shore themselves up against this mental aberration, many take refuge in faith in some supreme being who holds the key to all mysteries and the antidote to all suffering. In exchange for humility, God promises us knowledge, countering our painful multiplicity with his own soothing unity. But, if God existed, He would have made us in a different mould, either total prisoners of the matter from which he forged us, or else completely unshackled by thraldom to our minds: either his equals or his slaves. He would not have abandoned his creatures in this condition mid-way between damnation and beatitude, obliged to pursue divine perfection with the imperfect instruments of human knowledge. If God has need of our imperfections, of our limitations, then He is no better than we are. He is not God, but a demon, and all things proceed from His essential wickedness. In these times, it is true, it is easier to believe in a demon rather than in God. I, who have looked into the eyes of dying soldiers and glimpsed the world beyond, have seen nothing but pitch darkness. So, rather than imagining myself at the mercy of some spirit of evil, I prefer to believe that the universe is driven not by some all-powerful will, but by the random play of chemistry. The thousand substances of which it is composed clash and mingle each time they meet, and their reactions may be as measureless as a stellar explosion or as minuscule as electrolysis; as mighty as the splitting of the atom or as sublime as the flowering of a cherry tree. When everything has finally mixed and merged, when oxidoreduction is complete, when matter is made of nuclei as small as grains of sand but as heavy as this planet, and each electron is set upon its fatal course, then there will be peace in the universe. Peace and death.

Viipuri, 12 April 1944

Dear Sampo,

This is the first peaceful afternoon I've had since we arrived, and I am taking advantage of it to write this letter. We've been having a hard time of it. Our arrival in Viipuri was eventful, to say the least. It took us several days to set the refugee centre to rights – everything was in a state of utter neglect. The hospital is short of everything, including staff. We are expecting a delivery of medical equipment, but we also need blankets and camp beds, and fuel and goodness knows what else. We're in a permanent state of alarm; we're not far from the front, and those in the know say that there could be a Russian attack. Plans have already been made to evacuate the place, if necessary. Several families of peasants who'd been evacuated came back with the thaw; they've moved back into their farms, which they had abandoned after the Winter War, and they refuse to leave them yet again. They won't even come to collect their rations, they're so frightened of being kept here in the refugee centre. They say that the Russians have no reason to attack, that Viipuri is no concern of theirs. Some days ago we saw the last German divisions retreating, walking down streets between silent crowds. Apparently the Germans are now drawn up at Uhtua. Anyway, too far away from here to alarm the Russians. The second regiment of coastal artillery arrived at Viipuri yesterday, on its way through. The soldiers camped near the hospital; they were singing the *Porilaisten marssi*. And so I thought of you. I am taking the liberty of addressing you in the familiar form, because otherwise I couldn't speak as frankly as I would like. I behaved stupidly that night we met at the Kämp. War does strange things to time, it distorts reality. In war, everything seems temporary, transient. Perhaps that's why I felt the need to say things to you that I would have kept for a later stage of our friendship, had there been one. I was selfish – thinking only of myself. I'd only just told you my name, and already I was going all out, telling you about my silly adolescent games. It's partly to do with the fact that I'm a Red Cross Nurse, I just take it too far. I simply can't stop wanting to be of help. You know, something struck me the very day that you arrived, that January morning when I showed you to your bed in the visitors' quarters: the fear in your eyes. It wasn't the fear that I was used to seeing, the sort you see in the eyes of soldiers who are mortally wounded, or of the father who has lost his son. It was a fear beyond all reason, not rooted in this world. I still remember how you looked at me, seated on your bed, when I turned to look back at you as I walked down the corridor. I felt your pain and I wanted to be of help – another example of my urge to help others, cost what it may. That's why I went to see Koskela, to ask him to keep an eye on you. When I saw you at the Kämp, I felt reassured. I thought that you seemed better, that you had settled in, found your place among us. But I hadn't yet seen your eyes. The moment I got closer, I saw that that same fear was still there, as strong as ever. Then I was impertinent enough to think that perhaps some gesture of affection might break through that paralysing shell of pain. I hadn't yet understood that yours was a different kind of suffering. I've been thinking about it these last few days. It must be terrible not to have a past, not to remember your own childhood; and even worse not to be able to share this suffering with someone else. Because no one has ever come back from the place you've fallen headlong into. For me, my childhood is an old photo I always carry with me, just a close-up of when I was a gap-toothed ten-year-old little girl. But the dress I'm wearing in that faded old photograph, the rather hazy background with our big old country house, they are a mine of memories which leap out to greet me every time I look at it. I understand how painful such a lack of memories must be, how awful it must be to have nothing but emptiness behind you. But perhaps it is a mistake to keep on searching for a past which has now completely disappeared. After all, the past is in fact the only wound which always heals – indeed, it does so on its own, without any help from us. Is this compulsion to seek out traces of your past self really so strong? Would it not be more helpful to work patiently at filling in real time – that time which is left to you – building up a new memory for yourself brick by brick, as one might put it? An interfering friend might help to distract you from this obsessive search for something which has gone. Please write to me. Tell me how you spend your days. Tell me about Koskela's sermons. Does he still get so wound up? Tell me about Helsinki, now that spring is here. Has the new grass started coming up? Is the Esplanadi coming into leaf? Next month, the berries will be ripening in the woods. If they give me permission to come back, we'll go and gather them together.

Love,
Ilma

I had found this letter on my bed, when I went back to the dormitory to collect my notebook for my lesson with the pastor. It was the first time I'd seen my name on an envelope. It looked good, written there in black ink; so good that I almost didn't want to open it. I did not immediately understand all that I read. I rushed excitedly from one line to another, looking for words I knew and skipping those I felt I would be able to decipher later. Sometimes a few letters were enough to tell me all I needed to know about a verb and then a whole line would dance before me, the words opening out one after another, letting the meaning shine through. But often whole sentences remained unclear, clouded by very little words, like so many padlocks obstructing the flow of meaning. I read all that I could, then I curled up on the bed, holding the unfolded sheet of paper firmly in my hand. Weak sunlight fell through the window, slithering across the floors right up to the beds. The room was flooded with perfect silence, like still water, through which my body was slowly surfacing. Those words were bringing every part of me to life, enlarging me through their magnifying lens. Ilma had called out to my grief, had given it a name, and it was answering her call.

'I was expecting you. Are you not feeling well?'

It was Koskela; he was standing in the doorway.

'No, I'm fine, I'd just dozed off. I'm all yours.'

I got off the bed, picked up the notebook and straightened the blanket. The pastor pretended not to notice as I stuffed the letter into the pocket of my jacket. Then, without asking for any explanation, he answered the questions I put to him about the bits I had not understood, copied down into my notebook.

'Today we'll have our lesson in the open air. I want to show you something,' he said, striding off with his hands in his pockets. We went out into the road, came to the Suurtori and went down to the wharf at Katajanokka. The day was mild and colourless; a pearly light fell from the white sky, casting no shadows.

'There's something you need to understand: the frontier on which this war is being fought does not just divide two peoples, us and the Russians. It also separates two different souls. Sister souls, it's true, but tragically at odds on one

118

Diego Marani

essential point: the idea of the world to come. And for man, a mortal creature who lives a fleeting life upon this earth, the world to come is all-important.'

We had crossed the Katajanokka Canal in front of the presidential palace. Now we were climbing the hill on which the Uspenski Orthodox Cathedral stands. I tried to keep up with the pastor as he climbed the steep slope, the better to understand his words.

'That's typical of the Russians,' he said, stopping at the main door. Luckily he was out of breath, and this forced him to speak more slowly.

'Look how solidly it's built. Their truth is as heavy as stone, as conspicuous as those gilded domes, massive and down-to-earth. They named this church after the dormition of the Virgin. That's a myth of their own making, to spare the mother of God the brutal shock of physical death: it makes death into one endless sleep. A noble ruse, it's true. But if death is sleep, the world to come is just a dream, a fleeting vision.'

I did not know what *katoavainen* meant but, since he pronounced it next to *näky*, or vision, I could hazard a guess. I repeated the two words to myself to bind them to one another in my memory. We went into the church. The walls were crowded with images, the floor was elaborately worked and the altars were laden with gilded candlesticks, so that the cold light falling from above seemed to have a warmer glow, to be less harsh. We were surrounded by a circle of saints who looked down on us benevolently. Beneath each holy image, candles shone, their stems as slender as those of flowers. The steps leading to the niches were covered with red carpets. Elaborate brass lamps hung from the marble columns. We took a few steps in silence. Walking ahead of me, the pastor pointed to one picture, then another, then to the domes, with their coloured mosaics with scenes from the Old Testament. When we came out, the dull light hurt my eyes. The ethereal city stretched out below us, aloof and uncaring. We went down again towards the market square.

'You see, in the Orthodox World you are never alone. You end up by believing that when you go into the next world, you will be received into that crowd of welcoming saints and angels who are gathered there especially to meet you. They will keep you company until the Last Judgement, which, for the Orthodox, is nothing to be afraid of. It's just a rite of passage, a bit like the day when soldiers take the oath, nothing more. Then a new life will begin, exactly like this earthly one but without suffering, in a glittering many-splendoured earthly paradise. For the Orthodox, death does not exist and paradise is just like this world, with some slight alterations for the better.'

From the seashore we turned to look at the Uspenski Cathedral once more before turning down the Esplanadi. With some difficulty, one by one, I was taking in Koskela's words. In the pauses between them, I heard them die away. I watched them floating down into the landscape of the city around us, so as to note where they fell, so that I could go and collect them later: a belltower would remind me of a verb, I wasted a whole ship on an adjective and entrusted the all-important subject to a tram. The pastor's thought was scattered throughout Helsinki, and I could reread it every time I pleased.

'For us, however, there is no redemption. We grow up with a need for expiation and continue to punish ourselves throughout our lives. We entertain no hopes, make no demands. We are gobbets of pure evil, and the best thing we can do is to melt away, wither away, without any fuss. Only in the world to come will some of us be vouchsafed a way out. Nor do our actions serve to earn us any reward, for our fate is predestined.

Our damnation or salvation is already sealed, right from the day of our birth. But only after death will we know this. That is why our lives are just one stricken period of waiting.'

Lunastus, redemption, is a lovely word. I liked to repeat it to myself, to feel its mysterious murmur on my breath, as though some spirit were unleashed by those lisping sounds and set soaring upwards towards higher worlds. We had now crossed the Mannerheimintie; after walking in front of the Hotel Torni, we turned into the Lönrotinkatu. We went into a park, full of well-grown, shady trees, in the middle of which we could just make out a white building with a greenish roof. Here the pastor suddenly came to a standstill.

'That, on the other hand, is our soul. Look at these memorial tablets. They're all over the park.'

I looked around and noticed marble slabs set into the thick grass. Some crooked, others half sunk into the earth, they were thinly and discreetly scattered throughout the great stretch of grassy land.

'They're tombs; this is a cemetery. But it's also a park, where living people go to walk among the dead, This is our idea of the world to come: a place half a metre below ground, not a cheerful throng of saints. Nothing celestial or sublime about our world to come: it's a gloomy, colourless limbo where absence of guilt does duty for beatitude. Guilt is the wellhead of all that gives us life. We do not know what it is we feel guilty about, we have forgotten, it's not important any more. Perhaps it is just the guilt we feel at having come into the world at all. Eternal peace is liberation from guilt. Or, if you like, from life.'

A gust of wind swept through the trees, then ran along the grass. The weather was changing: a storm was brewing up. Above the sea the sky was still white and still, but black clouds

121

were rolling in from the west, and the park suddenly became dark. Beneath the trees the light began to fade, and the first raindrops pattered onto leaves which had now taken on silvery tones, like those of olive-trees.

'Come on, let's go into the church, at least we'll be in the dry,' said the pastor, pointing towards the white building we'd seen earlier. We ran towards the doorway and went into what turned out to be a Lutheran Church. It was built entirely of wood, a single space without nave or aisles. Once inside, Koskela stopped under the organ loft and pointed out a notice hanging on the wall. It had a red and black border, and looked somehow ominous. I tried to read it, but there were many words I did not know. I understood only bits of any one sentence, but nonetheless I gleaned an idea of the general meaning. It talked of mothers, suffering and the homeland. Even the title bristled with dishearteningly long words, studded with umlauts. But, taken letter by letter, the screws that held them so tightly in place began to yield, allowing some drop of meaning to seep out.

'This is a proclamation by Marshal Mannerheim, father of Finland, the man who led us out of Russia as Moses led the Israelites out of Egypt. It says that he is awarding every Finnish mother the Cross of Freedom, as compensation for the pain of having lost their sons in war. What a baffling title – *Ylipäällikön päiväkäsky*. Order of the day from the Commander-in-chief. But for those who can read between the lines, it's actually a war bulletin; and nowhere else in the world would you find a war bulletin posted up in a church. This proclamation was issued two years ago, on 10 May 1942, when the Finnish authorities had agreed to let the German troops go through their country on their way to launch a new attack on Leningrad. This was the beginning of our revenge; or of our ultimate defeat. At the end of hostilities with the Russians in 1940, we had had to accept extremely harsh conditions of surrender. Without having lost a single battle, with her army still intact, Finland was forced to hand over those very battlefields where her little fighting force had managed to stand up to the mighty military power of Soviet Russia. We had no choice. To have refused would have meant total annihilation. So Finnish provinces and cities had to be evacuated. There was a massive exodus from Karelia. Viipuri, Finland's second city, was emptied of its inhabitants and handed over to Russia. We have taken it back; but how long will we be able to hold on to it? We have always played for high stakes with the Russians, always bet heavily with nothing to fall back on. And, so far, this has paid off. At the time of the Bolshevik Revolution, Finland too was caught up in the civil war. Red and white Finns were massacred and exterminated so viciously that our country lay all but empty for decades. Even today we do not talk about those years, we do not mourn those who died, and many graves remain unmarked. Even today the military authorities are afraid that some of the soldiers who go off to defend our frontiers might be covert Reds, who would fraternize with the Soviets! We have taken a great gamble, we have risked our all! The victory of the Whites meant the survival of our nation, of our way of life, our God. If the Reds had won the civil war, if we had refused peace in 1940, today this place would be an army depot or a communist party headquarters. And the memorial tablets you saw out there would have ended up serving as paving for some city street. In reality, this 'proclamation' is an appeal, launched by Mannerheim to invite our people once again to risk their lives in the eternal struggle against the Russians. Accepting Hitler's help meant incurring Russia's fury and risking annihilation. Awarding the Cross of Freedom to Finland's mothers meant asking them to make the supreme sacrifice, giving their country even those sons who had survived, who had come unscathed through the Winter War. Their country was calling upon them once again. Marshal Mannerheim is the Väinämöinen of our time. He made Finland a free country, he saved us twice over: from the Reds and from the Russians. For us, these words come second only to the Bible. Do you see the difference? The Orthodox bow down before gilded images, we bow down before a typewritten order of the day! Now do you understand why we are two separate races?'

I was surprised at having understood almost all that the pastor had said. The words, I mean. As far as the politics were concerned, I was in no position to pass judgement, and I knew that he was often swept away by the sheer fervour of his vision. As in an unfamiliar forest, my mind had to make its own way as it went along. Whenever I lost the pastor from sight as I followed him on his frenetic ramblings, I had always managed to regain my bearings, to catch up with him again without too much difficulty, taking other paths. By now, in the discussions that had become the staple of our time together, I had acquired a reasonable mastery of his vocabulary, using my common sense as best I could, leaning limping words up against able-bodied ones in order to move forward. As Koskela walked before me towards the centre of the church, I noted with satisfaction how stark and unadorned the proclamation was, as indeed was the place where it was hung: not a single picture, not a single ornament on the whitewashed walls: except, in the middle of the apse, one single framed canvas, a Last Judgement where God the Father, with a white beard, was descending from a sulphurous heaven to separate men into sheep and goats. To the right were the damned, already licked by the flames of Hell, and to the left the blessed, a formless multitude clad in white tunics. Now Koskela had reached the altar. He made an expansive gesture, then spoke.

'Here no one is going to come forward to greet you; no saints, no cherubim. Here there are just black missals on the pews, and the numbers of the psalms hanging up on the walls. Our very church furnishings tell you what is important, that is, prayer. Because all in all it is the word of God which absolves or damns you. In Finnish, the word for Bible is *Raamattu*, that is, Grammar. Life is a set of rules. Beyond the rule lies sin, incomprehension, perdition.'

Outside, the storm was raging. The rain was beating down on the copper roof, drowning out the pastor's words. A sinister darkness now filled the empty church.

'At heart, we have always been Lutherans, even before we became Christians. The heroes of the *Kalevala* were already Lutherans in the same way that Achilles and Ulysses were already Orthodox. Ulysses practised his wiles on a sophisticated and sceptical society which was familiar with mental trickery. Väinämöinen's mode of speech is craggy, immediate, uncomplicated, like the first blow of a chisel on rough stone. The Greek gods mingled with men, wrangled and negotiated with them. The god Ukko never comes down to earth; he judges our actions and then visits light or darkness upon us, punishment or reward. The fate of the Greeks is erratic, ironical; it makes great warriors of simple men. Its will seems to be inescapable, yet it can in fact be outmanoeuvred. The destiny that awaits the Finnish heroes is brutal, inflexible. It turns great warriors into simple shepherds who serve out their sentence until the very last.'

Koskela was becoming carried away by his own words. He had laid his clenched fists upon the altar and was now preparing to give one of his own special sermons. Lucid passion shone forth from his lean face; or was it madness? I could now longer follow what he was saying, but his expression kept me rooted to the spot, the tone of his voice commanded my attention.

'Väinämöinen and his companions were surprised by just such a storm when they were fleeing from the land of Pohjola after having stolen the *Sampo*. The fury of the waves had driven them to the edges of the world. For days and days they had sailed over a sea with no horizon; now it loomed up before them from the dark mist bit by bit, at every stroke of the oar. Then they found the route home. The green line of the coast led them towards the land of Kaleva. But they did not know that the mistress of Pohjola was pursuing them on a ship rowed by a hundred oarsmen, defended by a thousand armed men. When the *runoilija* realized that the shadow in the midst of the sea was not just another island emerging briefly from the waves, but the ship of the mistress of Pohjola, bristling with swords and lances, he was truly afraid that his last hour had come. Equally alarmed, his companions looked in his direction, waiting for some word, for some decision. From the nearby shore, shrouded in mist, a thousand startled pheasants took to the air. All the fish in the sea took refuge in the deepest waters, where the rock is warm, and cloaked with the red seaweed which feeds the monsters who live below the earth's crust.'

I had at last managed to begin to make some sense of the well-known tales of old Finnish mythology. Koskela became easier to understand when he opened his book of such stories. Describing the characters from the *Kalevala*, he would imitate their features, mime their voices. I had no time mentally to register words that I did not know, but Koskela's face and gestures helped me to recognize the character he was talking about. I could visualize the page of the book where he was represented, and the things around him, too, took on similar colouring. As to the ships and weapons, Koskela imitated them so well that I didn't even try to pinpoint the word which described them. I knew I would be able to track it down at a later stage, recognizing it from the pastor's gestures.

'His hands around the thole-pin, Väinämöinen watched the ship approach, saw the swords sparkling. Already he could hear the warriors' cries. The old *runoilija* closed his eyes so that the words to be sung would come into his mind; then he rose to his feet, took a knife from his knapsack, hacked off a piece of flint and threw it into the sea, saying: "May a black rock spring up from this stone, a submerged rock which will destroy Pohjola's ship, which will split its hull like a knife ripping through the white belly of a toad!' Then the water seethed, the waves parted in a gigantic maelstrom, and a peak of rock surfaced like a sea monster, instantly to be hidden by the waves. Väinämöinen heaved a sigh of relief. Once again the sea, his erstwhile mother, had come to his aid. The three heroes stopped rowing and listened in silence. Creaking majestically, Pohjola's ship sailed on, breasting the waves securely to the helmsman's call, when suddenly a blow sent the masts crashing downwards into the sea. The timbers shattered upon the rock, the freezing water poured into her warm belly, and she sank from sight.'

The rumble of the thunder, and the blaze of lightning visible through the church's high skylights served as a powerful backdrop to Koskela's narrative. Important words were lost to me in the din, even as I sought to decipher them on the pastor's lips. But then I gave myself over to watching him as he rowed through the mighty waves unleashed by Väinämöinen's magic. I somehow sensed that in one of the many lives a shaman is

127

vouchsafed, the pastor had been on board that ship. Perhaps it was not a legend he was telling, but a memory from his own youth.

'Clinging to the rock, the mistress of Pohjola looked on in terror as her ship sank and her soldiers disappeared into the waves like bits of useless iron. Then she laid hold of five rusty scythes and five twisted hooks, and turned them into talons which she bound on to her hands. She collected the timbers and made them into huge wings, cut out a tail for herself from the sails, fashioned herself a pointed beak from the mizen-mast, into which she drove sharp nails. She placed a thousand archers on one wing, a thousand armed men on the other and hurled herself at Väinämöinen's boat. Seeing the monstrous bird that was throwing itself upon him, Väinämöinen raised his eyes to the heavens and said: "Mighty Ukko, you alone can save us". But the valorous Lemminkäinen rose to his feet, unsheathed his sword and severed the talons of the monstrous bird with a single downward stroke; then he hacked its wings into pieces, and the thousands of archers and armed men hurtled into the sea and disappeared in the black water. The mistress of Pohjola, clinging to the three heroes' boat, flung herself upon the magic *Sampo* and clasped it to herself, but it slipped out of her hands and fell into the sea. She tried to regain her hold of it, but managed only to seize one of its lids. Heavy as a mountain, the *Sampo* sank down into the sea and shattered into a thousand pieces on the warm rock of the sea bottom, where the red seaweed grows. Suddenly the waves froze, the fish became nothing but white bones and stone birds plummeted down from a smoke-filled sky. Nothing moved. Life had disappeared from the face of the earth. The god Ukko had sucked it all back into himself. The magic *Sampo* had been destroyed, and darkness had once more taken possession of the earth.'

He had spoken without drawing breath. Now he was looking puzzledly at the dark nave, as though he had forgotten where he was. He stepped down from the altar, shaking back the hair which had fallen over his eyes and came to sit beside me on the bench. The downpour that was falling on to the oval of glass above the door cast a teeming shadow on the floor.

'The right word. That's all the difference between life and death. Memory is inseparable from words. Words draw things out of the shadows. Learn the words and you will recover your memory,' were his last words before he fell silent. Head in his clasped hands, he seemed not even to be breathing. I cannot be sure of this, but it seemed to me that he had his eyes wide open and was staring fixedly into the darkness. Drunk on his words, tired after our long walk, I too was dozing off. I dreamed that I was surrounded on all sides by a fretful, silent crowd which was dragging me with it on its random course. Someone, swept along by the mass, had their arms around my neck so as to avoid being trampled under foot. I felt their spasmodic grip, their nails upon my skin, and I woke up with cramp in the upper part of my back. Leaning over to one side, I had collapsed on to the bench. Aching all over, legs and arms numb, I straightened up; the pastor was standing in front of me.

'The storm is over, let's go,' he said without any sign of emotion, and set off for the door of the church, hands clasped behind his back.

This is the first time that I have read an account of the events of our civil war told through the eyes of a Finn. I lost my father in that war, and today he does not even have a grave where I can go to mourn; I find it hard to endorse certain patriotic myths, and it grieves me, but also enrages me, that this sometimes causes me to pass for a traitor. Often, even within one single people, the fatherland will be riven into groups, each failing to acknowledge the other; and it is this that lies at the root of the madness which has reduced Europe to ashes. Despots masquerading as patriots insist on the importance of their own myths, proclaiming that, without such myths, there can be no true patriotism. Thus the fatherland is reduced to a matter of borders, proclaimed as sacred above all other contending ones, sometimes in the name of the same god. The leaders who today are boasting of having reunified a Finland formerly divided into Reds and Whites, fail to see that they have carved a deep rift within our people. They claim to have made Finland whole again; yet the men shot without trial by Mannerheim's white guards were part of the country too. One day someone will have to have the courage to wrest the monopoly of the fatherland from these impostors and give it back to all free men, to those who draw up frontiers with ideas and not with barbed wire. Essentially, the fatherland is the land of your fathers, but my father is dead and I am the son of others, enrolled by force in the German army to fight a war which was not my own. There is no longer any fatherland in which I can believe.

I had never realized that the word Raamattu *derived from Grammar. It is one of those things that is so utterly obvious that you fail to notice them. Yet perhaps it tells us a lot about the Finns' own deep love of their own language. For us, language is the word of God, even when you don't believe in Him, and grammar is an exact science, made up of commensurable meanings and based on unquestionable theorems. The right word gives thought a sense of harmony, the mathematical inevitability of music. But each age plays different music, and chords which were once regarded as the work of the devil no longer frighten anyone. There is no such thing as eternal harmony: like everything else in this world, sounds too have their day, and man has to invent new ones in order to ward off silence. What we today regard as music would have been seen as noise a hundred years ago. Yesterday's mistake is just today's harmless oddity. The rule always succeeds the word: this is the great weakness of all grammar. The rule is not order, it is just a description of some form of disorder. Like everything peculiar to man, language too changes, and to strive for linguistic purity is as senseless as to strive for its racial equivalent. Linguists say that all languages tend towards simplification, aiming to express the maximum of possible meaning through the fewest possible sounds. So the shortest words are also the oldest, the most worn away by time. In Finnish, the word for war is* sota, *and these two syllables are eloquent pointers to how many we have indeed waged.*

A language's prescriptive baggage comes into being less to facilitate its comprehension, than to prevent foreigners' access to it. Each language barricades itself behind the hard won knowledge of its grammar, like a secret sect behind its mumbo-jumbo. But language is not a religion in which one can believe or not believe. Language is a natural phenomenon, peculiar to all humanity. Human stupidity has divided it up into a plurality of grammars, each claiming to be the 'right' one, to reflect the clarity of thought of a whole people. Thus each people learns the rules of its own grammar, deluding itself that it is these same rules that will resolve life's mysteries.

Ever since Finland had refused the peace conditions laid down by the Russians, the spectre of war had returned to haunt Helsinki. Just as it was beginning to recover from the February bombings, the city was once more plunged into a state of fear. Troop movements began. In the wan spring sunshine, the green uniforms of the frontier guards patrolling the Suurtori, their blue and white cockades a-flutter, had something cheerful yet also grimly determined about them. Trains laden with troops and cannon manoeuvred laboriously in front of the harbour before finally moving off, whistling lugubriously. The bay filled up with warships, looming up suddenly from the archipelago and coming to anchor offshore, where they remained, as motionless as whales. The Kämp itself was a sea of activity. Many new faces had arrived, receiving haughty treatment from the old-timers. The questions they asked showed that they knew nothing about the country, let alone the city. On foot, they never ventured beyond the Esplanadi, and went around exclusively in taxis, even just for a few hundred metres. They seemed irritated by the fact that nothing was yet happening, and spent their mornings in the hotel press-room, glued to the telephone with their reports. A rumour was going around to the effect that the Russians were preparing a landing. At the slightest press leak, taxis packed with journalists would dash out of the city and head in the direction of some distant bay, awaiting ships which never came. Once I accompanied my journalist friend on one of these forays. We went through Porvoo and carried on the road to Kotka, rounding a promontory with a lighthouse and driving down towards the sea. Kilometre after kilometre had gone by without our encountering a living soul. Immediately inland from the coast, the woods began, approached by a stony track across a field. We positioned ourselves at the side of the road, enjoying the weak sunlight.

The beach was strewn with rock spikes, stuck into the sand point upwards, to prevent panzers from landing. The reporters had their cameras at the ready; one American journalist had even brought his binoculars. We waited endlessly, in silence, like hunters on the *qui vive*. The landscape stretching before us had something curiously geometrical about it: the white beach, with its rocky prisms drawn up in tidy ranks, the glassy slabs of sky and sea, welded together by the line of the horizon, crisp and watertight. Some time in the middle of the afternoon, everything changed colour: the blue of the sea deepened, the blue of the sky faded to white and the rock spikes ceased to cast a shadow. Some people went down on to the beach and began strolling along it, kicking idly at the shells. Others went back to the taxi, and asked the driver to take them back to a shop they'd passed on their way, to get something to drink. The reporters had put down their cameras and were sitting on the sand, having a smoke. A wind got up, soughing through the wood behind us. We ended the afternoon throwing stones at an empty barrel bobbing in the water, and at sunset we set off again for Helsinki.

'I expect we'll find the Russians waiting for us at the Kämp,' joked someone as we piled back into the car.

With May came light. They put little tables out at Kappeli's, and in the morning fishing boats would tie up at the wharves in front of the market, selling salt fish and onions. The ferry to the islands came back into action, a little old wooden steamer smelling of diesel and wet rope. It would make a languid departure at mid-day, taking a broad turn in the bay before disappearing behind the island where the yacht club was. The days were pulling out, and all that light would send me wandering the streets till late, almost always on foot, stopping to rest on the benches when I was well and truly exhausted.

Sometimes I would board the first tram that came along and go on to discover new parts of the city. By now I'd been through every suburb of Helsinki, from Laakso to Valilla. Koskela had given me a map which he'd torn out of the telephone directory, putting pencil rings around the places I should visit. A conscientious tourist, I had been to every single one, always bringing back some memento, a theatre programme, a ticket I'd found on the ground, an empty packet of some unknown brand of cigarette. I took notes, followed my routes on the map, copied out words I had not understood, and had the pastor explain them to me during the next lesson. Day after day, I had gradually taken possession of Helsinki's streets. I began to sample the reassuring feeling of already knowing what awaited me round the next corner. Like an animal on its own home ground, I had dug my own personal itineraries out of the tangle of streets, the routes I took to go from one place to another without bothering to try and find the shortest one. But I knew the city as a tourist, not as a native.

The moment anyone asked me anything, no matter how banal, my reassuring sense of anonymity deserted me. My words betrayed my outsider status: my very voice gave off sounds that did not ring true, like a cracked glass. The language did not flow with ease; I had to construct each word carefully before pronouncing it, laboriously seeking the right amount of breath, the correct pressure of the lips, sounding out my palate with my tongue in search of the only point which could produce the sound I was looking for and then turning it into the right case before actually delivering it up. That cavity which was my mouth, which seemed so small, would suddenly become immense. It seemed impossible to me that everything should be played out within those fractions of a millimetre, that a segment of muscle, if too tense, should alter a meaning completely, that one puff of air too much, or too little, should be enough to cause me to be mistaken for an Estonian or Ingrian, or indeed break off the thread of meaning entirely.

Often on the tram I would pick up bits of phrases, snatches of conversation which I would brood over mentally until I learned them. Then, when I was alone, stretched out on my bed before falling asleep, I would repeat them aloud, building up the missing parts around them and projecting invented worlds on to the grey walls of the visitors' quarters, in which I would engage in conversation with imaginary friends to whom I gave the faces of the people who had been around me in the tram. When Koskela left, and I was absolutely alone, I could no longer distinguish real people from those I had imagined. One day, at the no.7 tram stop, I said a friendly hello to an elderly gentleman with a moustache who had showed me the way to the Olympic Stadium not long before. Only later did I realize that I had imagined the whole thing or, to be more accurate, that I had muddled things up: the gentleman with the moustache had given the relevant information not to me, but to a young man sitting next to me on the tram; and it wasn't the Olympic Stadium he'd wanted, but the university hospital. The Olympic Stadium was what I could see out of the tram window at that moment. I remembered every one of the words they had exchanged, the expressions and even the gestures that had gone with them. Like so many others, I had repeated them a thousand times: I had made them my own.

In my wanderings, I would mingle with the silent crowds leaving church on a Sunday, or with the queues outside the grocers' shops. I also liked to join the throng of people boarding a tram: I would pretend that I too was getting off at a certain stop, that I too was going somewhere specific, and from time to time I would look out of the window to see how far it was to my imagined destination. Then I would get off at some randomly chosen street, walk purposefully for ten or twenty paces, to give the tram time to move off, then resume my aimless ramblings. I would go on to the next stop and wait for the tram on the other side of the street, taking it back where I had come from. To all intents and purposes I was a Finn like all those around me, except that no one knew me; six months ago, no one would have seen me. They greeted one another, recognized each other when they met. I was not included in any handshake. If all the inhabitants of Helsinki had come together one day to talk about that lonely individual with the strange accent who walked from one end of the city to the other at the strangest hours, getting on and off trams at random, they would have found that not one of them knew me, that not one of them knew where I was from.

But if human beings were unacquainted with me, inanimate things on the other hand – gardens, trams and buildings – knew me well. I often caught myself addressing the curious-looking houses in Eira, with their rounded roofs and floral balustrades. With them, I didn't need to worry about my pronunciation – I could greet them in Finnish like old friends. I would tell them where I was going, what I had been doing; they bore their names carved or painted on their façades, and I would speak them out loud. I felt particularly happy talking to the trees on the Esplanadi – after all, they were the ones that knew me best. But I talked to them under my breath, so that no one would hear me engaging so closely, and oddly, with another species. Beneath their branches, I felt safe; I found it reassuring to see that they were now so luxuriant, to know that they were well and truly alive in all their silent greenery. I felt their roots spreading beneath my feet, retaking possession of the earth which had been frozen for so many months, and this too gave me heart. Then the white nights came: punishing sunsets would slowly trickle into dawns as dense as drops of mercury. With that never-darkening sky outside, it was impossible to stay indoors. The night light flooded the city with its white silence, suffusing every room, however shut away, reaching down into the deepest cellars, unearthing people wherever they lay hidden and driving them outside. Wandering through the streets, crossing the bay from side to side, as far as the encircling forests, they set out in pursuit of the mirage of eternity which those undying days seemed falsely to promise. Goaded on by this same ungovernable lunacy, I too would go out to contemplate the disquieting yet majestic sight of darkness becoming light. I liked above all to walk along the beach, beyond the bay of Taivallahti. The sea itself seemed to be in thrall to that same magic. Perhaps this was the world of the heroes of the *Kalevala*; perhaps it had never come to an end, was still living on beside our own, visible only to shamans like the Pastor Koskela. Caught up in such fantasies, I imagined ships laden with warriors emerging from the sea, glittering and bristling with lances. I saw the tree trunks scattered on the beach as so many gruesome idols, the lightning flashing out at sea as the limitless wrath of the god Ukko. Those night-time hours, stolen from sleep, truly belonged to another era, another world, and you needed to be very drunk to embrace the sense of infinity they bore so numinously in their wake.

More than a month had gone by since I had received Ilma's letter. Ever since that afternoon, I'd kept it in the inner pocket of my jacket, where I kept the handkerchief with my initials. I had reread it a thousand times until I had learned it by heart, and I had only to come across a verb, an adjective, even just a pair of prepositions in my notebook for a whole line of it to flash into my mind. I had asked Koskela about every single word I had not understood. I had made an orderly list of them in my notebook and, in order to be sure that nothing that Ilma had said escaped me, I had looked into their most far-fetched and most unlikely meanings. Time after time, before falling asleep at night, I had been tempted to reply. I had begun to sketch out a few phrases in my mind: 'Dear Ilma, all that you say is true,' I would begin, but could never go any further. I slipped the second letter to arrive into the same pocket as I had put the first, but a whole day went by before I could bring myself to open it. Only in the evening, after I'd filled myself with *koskenkorva* at the Kämp, did I walk to the hill in Kaivopuisto Park and there, under the tree of happy memories, now in full leaf, I unstuck the envelope and began to read.

Viipuri, 22 May 1944

Dear Sampo,

I am saddened by your silence, but all in all I am not surprised. Because I was presumptuous enough to think that I could help you, I thrust a friendship upon you that may have been unwelcome, and I must accept your rejection of it. In reality it is I who need you, and once again I misjudged matters. What you need is a past, whereas what I need is a present, something to distract me from the fear and anxiety with which I live. Don't read these words thinking that I want to help you yet again. I am not asking for a reply; just let me write to you. With you – and in reality I know nothing about you except your name – I feel an unusual sense of intimacy which is somehow liberating and life-enhancing; it's also something I've never felt with people I thought that I knew well. Thinking of you gives me a new lightness, lets me float free of the ballast of memory. Strangely, what you are so doggedly in search of drags me down, it is a form of slavery to which I cling. What others remember of us is in fact nothing more than the effect that we have had on them. We spend our lives brushing up against our fellow humans without ever really knowing them. Even the knowledge we build up of those people and things which are dearest to us is purely matter-of-fact; we know them as the entomologist knows the butterflies he has pinned on to a sheet of balsa wood. We can describe the colour of their eyes or hair, we know them from a distance as they walk through a crowd, their features are instantly recognizable, as is their characteristic smell, or voice. Their absence makes us feel some part of us is missing. Yet they are never truly ours: our wish to possess them in fact destroys them, denies them a life of their own. In our vain desire to soften the mystery of death, we seek to possess, to soak up as much life as we can, without realizing that in this way we are killing all that we think we love. Do you remember my tree in Kaivopuisto Park? There are many ways of seeing it: you can regard it as a network of lymph vessels, of veins, of roots teeming with sap, linked up to a living nucleus which, through the breathing leaves, establishes and maintains a flow of matter between earth and sky, between inert matter and air. But you can also reduce it to a pure number, make it into a law of chemistry which governs the way things decompose and are transformed. In both cases, different though they are, that tree will still be something outside ourselves, something we are observing, something we know, perhaps, but with which we do not have any relationship. Establishing a relationship, that's what we're talking about: agreeing to move towards the other without taking possession of them, without making them conform to what we expect of them. That's what I'd like to do with you. Only with you could such a relationship be possible – for the simple reason that there is nothing I can steal from you. When two people meet, they immediately want to 'declare' their past, as you declare alcohol and cigarettes at a frontier post: they want to 'clear' it, to put it at the disposal of the new relationship on which they are embarking. But that's not the right way to go about things; it's simply a rather presumptuous way of claiming a right to the other person's past by scraping together memories which are not our own. You yourself have no past, so you have no memory to put at anyone's disposal. My tree of happy memories, on the other hand, is a monument of self-centredness, a weight which drags me down. Did you ever go back to it? It must be all in leaf by now. There you are – I belittle it and then immediately wish I hadn't done so! Without someone else beside us, watching us live, we might as well be dead, and there is no point in plundering the past in the vain hope of wresting its treasure from it, because that is treasure that cannot be spent, counterfeit coinage no one will accept. Life has to be spent right away, consumed on the spot, while it's still warm, like the grilled whitefish and spring onions you get on the market square. Have you been to the market? Are they selling flowers there yet? Last summer, there was always a little old woman selling flowers near the place where the ferry from the islands comes in; never more than two or three bunches, tied up with string, which she'd put into margarine drums filled with water. I always liked to buy a bunch – not so much for the flowers themselves, but to see the smile that would light up her eyes when I put the coin into her hand. Here, spring has not brought much of a let-up: the flowers in the fields, the new green of the woods, the tang drifting in from the open sea, driving away the stench of the dried mud – they can't do much for us. In fact, all this light is an insult to our black fear; we no longer have the dark to hide away in. The Russians are so near that on windy nights it's as though we could hear their voices through the rustling of the leaves. We expect to see them leaping out of the woods – first one by one, then in their droves, in silent cohorts, as multitudinous as only they could ever be – then spreading in their hordes throughout the city. Perhaps it's this sense of vulnerability which makes me so unguarded, so open to new possibilities. It's at moments like this, when there's nothing more to lose, that we feel the need to love every human being around us as though they were a part of us, as though our people were a single body and each of us one of its muscles, its limbs, its organs. Sampo – you whom I do not know – today I want to ask you not to forget me, not to abandon me. If you don't want to write to me, at least think of me. I'll know that you are doing so, and that will be enough. It will help me get through these hard times, to keep alive the dream that one day I may find you again.

With all my love,

Ilma.

Recognizing her writing brought me comfort. Written in that hand, even the words I didn't know became almost comprehensible. I had not known that *hyönteistietelijaä* meant entomologist, but it appeared almost next to *perhosia*, meaning butterfly, so I could make the link. I even wondered whether Ilma had tried to construct her metaphors using words she thought that I would know. Of course I sensed her bitterness; it was quite clear that she was hurt, and I felt a deep pang of shame, a sudden desire to reach out towards her and offer my help, or at least write back to her. But then everything would get sucked back into the soft abyss of my inertia. To reach out to her meant coming out into the open, taking possession of a destiny I did not feel to be my own, a destiny I felt I was usurping. My lot was to be found wanting; I had to do penance for my name, wherever that might take me. I resealed the envelope and put it back in my pocket. The tree of memories rustled above my head, the silvery veins of its leaves caught in the light as they moved. I carried on sitting there, lost in thought; indeed, I must have fallen asleep, because when I woke up I could no longer distinguish between my thoughts and my dreams. How much time had gone by? Stiff with cold, I looked in the direction of the wind: to the west, the sea had become almost black, as though it had drunk up the darkness which the sky was lacking. Lightning flickered in the distance, but there was no thunder. In the amber-coloured light, the city below me was waking, without having slept. Exhausted by lack of sleep, I was breathing heavily. The windows of the houses looked like bruised eyes, the empty streets were corridors choked by polluted air. A red gash, short but deep as a wound, had opened up in the colourless sky to the east: dawn. Or Viipuri, burning.

Back in town, I learned that the Russians had attacked the Finnish positions on the Karelian Isthmus: the dreaded counter-attack had begun. The Kämp was in a state of ferment. A number of journalists and reporters were ready for the front; gathered together in the press-room with their luggage, they were impatiently waiting their turn for a taxi. In the bar, the newsreader was listing the places already under attack and the enemy formations and Finnish regiments involved, all in a suitably martial tone. A small crowd had come in to listen. At each name, faces darkened, some people were weeping, others were staring blankly and silently into the middle distance. Hotel porters, bar attendants, telephonists, all had deserted their posts to cluster round the loudspeaker; even the waiters had stopped moving among the tables. I too got caught up in the excitement, joining the knots of people commenting upon the latest news. A reporter with a camera round his neck came in, shouting. A rumour promptly circulated to the effect that a German ship with anti-tank shells had come into the port, and others were expected. A few nights earlier, I myself had noticed that a vessel bearing the flag of the German navy was moored alongside the quay in the harbour at Pohjoissatama, indeed I had stopped to inspect it more closely; it reminded me of the Tübingen. The photographer who'd just come in said he was convinced that German troops were about to land in Finland to launch a counter-offensive on Leningrad, but several officers who were standing outside the main huddle intervened to put paid to that rumour, explaining that here we were talking about military aid: Germany was arming Finland against a Russian attack, as had already happened in the first years of the war. An elderly man standing beside me made certain observations concerning this piece of news, shaking his head the while, then wandered off; someone made a disobliging comment. I too wanted to have my say, and found myself suddenly strangely talkative. I said that German aid was manna from Heaven – I was very proud of that expression, which I had learned from Koskela. A young man behind me came forward to declare himself in agreement, and this served to embolden me further: quickened by my excitement, the sentences built themselves up mechanically in my mind, the right words presented themselves effortlessly and I was amazed to hear myself pronouncing them; my Finnish was no longer a blend of sounds now spiky, now indistinct. Even if I still had trouble with my cases, the phrases which now came out of my mouth were clear-cut, well-turned. People were listening to me, some were nodding; for a moment I felt capable of chairing a meeting, but then I was distracted by other voices and abandoned my new-found role of orator to return to my more normal line of duty, helping some foreign journalists to explain to a taxi-driver where they wanted to go, telling some new arrival where the Russian attack had taken place, explaining to another what they were talking about at the bar. Then, propelled by another surge of excitement, I found myself wandering about the streets. A long column of troop-bearing trucks had formed on the Esplanadi, near the market square; youthful faces were peering out from under the tarpaulins. Bemused and baffled at having been thrust by history into the midst of such momentous times, they greeted the passers-by with a mixture of gravity and delight. The rhythmical sound of the engines, the metallic din they made in that square, normally so peaceful, was reminiscent of the hammering of cannon on a battlefield. Despite the bright sunlight, the city seemed to be in mourning; people were wandering aimlessly about the streets, drawn to any commotion, any crowd, scanning the light-filled streets, retailing accounts of unlikely events which they themselves did not believe. I wandered around for quite some time, as aimless as the rest, idly drawn to any group I came across. Some hours later I went back towards the market square, where the traders were packing up their stalls, tarpaulins swollen by the mild sea breeze. I sat down on the quay, away from the crowds, near the point where the ferry left for the islands; I was breathless with exhaustion, and the sun hurt my eyes. I would have liked to go home and sleep, but the very thought of the visitors' quarters made me feel uneasy: I wouldn't have been able to bear the smell of the disinfectant, the silence, broken by slight noises, the distant clatter and above all the daylight and attendant shadows on the walls. Looking again towards the square, I saw Ilma's flower seller leaning against a bollard, surrounded by her improvised containers. That was a pleasant surprise: I bought a bunch of wild flowers, watching her carefully as I handed her the coins, but I did not receive the expected smile. She thanked me humbly and lowered her eyes to stare at the cobbles, embarrassed by my insistent gaze. Truly exhausted now, I decided to go back to the hospital anyway. To avoid going straight into the visitors' quarters, I decided to put the flowers on the altar in the chapel; it wasn't yet mid-day, and the place was empty. There too the sunlight created a mood of misplaced optimism: usually sunk in smoke-filled gloom, the veining of the wood was suddenly revealed, like that on a delicate skin unaccustomed to light. I went into the sacristy and took out some sheets of writing paper I'd found in the Kämp. 'Dear Ilma', I began to write; but there I stopped; weariness drew my head down to the table, and I slept.

I did indeed find several sheets of writing paper in the middle of the notebook with the Kämp's letterhead, bearing different dates and just the words 'Dear Ilma', gone over several times to the point of tearing holes in the paper, always a sign that the writer does not know what to say next. Only one bore any other words: 'I know you're right, but I ...' written in a hesitant hand, then nothing. Only a heart of stone could have been left untouched by words like those in Miss Koivisto's letters. I wonder whether the author of these pages had fully understood their meaning. But the careful copyings out, the lists of verbs and nouns, the constant repetition, in other parts of the notebook, of expressions taken from her letters, give me cause to believe that in fact he did. Indeed, I am convinced that at a certain moment that man was actually preparing himself to write some reply. Perhaps he was discouraged by the difficulty of expressing his feelings in a language he had by no means fully mastered. But some things can be said quite simply, and sometimes a postcard with a simple greeting means more than a love letter. What is more likely, as Miss Koivisto herself maintains, is that that man was so obsessed by his search for his own identity that he was really at his wits' end. After Koskela's departure, left entirely on his own, the author of this document gradually lost all contact with reality. What is more the pastor, who must have been aware that his pupil was entertaining vague thoughts in connection with some woman, seems to have done nothing to encourage him to pursue them further, nor to support him in his efforts to forge for himself the sort of everyday life which turns the makeshift into something more permanent. Koskela was already caught up in the delirium which was ultimately to lead him to his end. The way he talked, his vision of the world, his merciless cynicism were already pulling him in the direction of his final choice, setting him on a path which was bound to lead to self-destruction. So Miss Koivisto's poignant words fell upon stony ground, that of a mind unravelling; his attempts to answer her may have been his last moments of lucidity.

Long, long ago, I too believed in promises that are written down on notepaper. Deluding myself that I would keep them, I covered fragile sheets of paper with feelings that were bigger than myself, that I thought I could master simply because I was able to write them down. In fact, here too I was behaving like a scientist: I described my state of mind just as I would have the symptoms and course of a disease. I had not yet realized that nothing that concerns man ever happens the same way *twice, that nothing is made to last and that the feelings by which I was being carried away would be vastly outlived by the organs which were producing them. I declared myself in love with the same lightness of heart with which certain of my patients declared that they had tuberculosis, as though TB were not some serious pulmonary pathology but a sort of state of mind. Like them, I was not aware of the seriousness of my illness. Indeed, it seemed to me that, written down, the awesome phenomenon by which I was beset would be more easily tamed, become more rational. I thought, wrongly, that my feelings, if written down on paper, would take on more solid form, and that such solidity would communicate itself to the person who read my letters. But one day, quite unexpectedly, words – set on their course long before I could read them – reached me, and killed me. Of all the types of cruelty that the person who loves us may inflict upon us, even without meaning to, this is the worst.*

At Hamburg, one autumn evening on my way back from the university, I had stopped to watch the sunset over the port. It was unusually mild for the time of year; the windows of the city were glowing red, the tram lines were a tangle of strips of blazing colour. Suddenly, in the pearly sky to the east, I saw a silent flock of migrating storks; soon they were above me, majestically large. Their shadow slipped over me like an embrace: up there in the soft air, the sight of them gave me a sudden feeling of peace. I gazed out over the iron-grey sea and allowed the beloved face of the girl I had left behind me in Helsinki to surface in my mind: I offered up that moment, that sunset, that flight of storks, to her. Some weeks later, I received a letter: words dry as thorns informed me, with brutal accuracy, how all that she had once felt for me was well and truly over. The date at the top of the letter, and the time of

day, mentioned in the first few lines, told me that the words
which were now crushing me had been written on the very
evening that I had seen the storks. At the very moment I had
been offering up that burst of joy to her, she had been signing
my death sentence.

One evening in June, the pastor went away. He told me nothing
about his intentions; indeed, he told nobody. He left no word,
no message. From the surprise and bewilderment caused in
the hospital by his departure I realized that he had long ceased
to communicate with his colleagues on the medical staff, and
indeed with the wounded whom he visited daily. He would
talk to them, they said, but did not listen: it was as though
he was always talking to the same person, carrying on with
what he was saying to one when moving on to talk to the next.
He seemed to speak in riddles, about a God whom he never
referred to by name but whose end he sensed to be imminent;
he had cut himself off from the world and lived like a castaway,
alone with his thoughts, so that to leave was the most natural
thing he could have done, an action which was quite simply
the last step in a long and anguished process of estrangement.
   Although I understood this only later, on his last evening
the Military Chaplain Olof Koskela had in fact taken his leave
of me, after his fashion. After the service I had blown out the
candle on the altar and tidied away the missals, as I always did.
The dread of yet another white night was looming; I lingered
on among the pews, taking a little bite out of the endless hours
when I was supposedly asleep. When I had done everything
there could possibly be to do, when I had exhausted every
excuse for further loitering, I went to the door of the sacristy to
say goodnight to the pastor. I found him seated at the table, with
the *Kalevala* open in front of him, the coloured illustrations

glowing in the light of the setting sun. The little cupboard with the glass knobs was open and the bottle of *koskenkorva* was on the table, together with two small glasses, just as it always was during our lessons. Without further ado, I went in; Koskela waited for me to sit down. In the past, each time he had begun to speak, I would concentrate on his words, ever hopeful that I would understand him; and indeed, with time and practice, my understanding of his Finnish had broadened and deepened. But it was above all at the beginning of any speech, before I could tell where it was going, that I would surprise myself by leaping from one phrase to another without losing my balance. Words and thought ran straight as a pair of rails, and I would feel the engine of grammar springing smoothly and harmoniously into motion. But the higher he clambered up the steep slopes of his cosmogony, the harder I had to struggle to follow him. Sometimes, noticing that I was in difficulties, he would reformulate certain ideas in simpler terms; as time went by, however, less aware of my plight, he ceased to do so. So that night too I sat down in front of the pastor with my eyes fixed on his mouth, so as not to let one single movement of his lips escape me.

'It was Väinämöinen, the great *runoilija*, who made a people of us. Before that we had been uncivilized, without a history, nomads who abandoned their dead wherever they happened to be. Väinämöinen gave us a land, taught us the art of working iron, the art of war, how to hunt and to grow crops. But there was just one thing Väinämöinen knew he could not do for us, namely, prevail over the evil that is inherent in all the things of this world: against that we are powerless, we and all other human beings. That was what Väinämöinen was thinking about on the evening of the great summer festival. After the hunt, while the bear meat was roasting in the coals, during the preparations for the great feast in celebration of the return of summer, of coots to the skies and salmon to the rivers, Väinämöinen was thinking back on his past life. The heroic age which had witnessed his birth was now long gone. Single-handedly he had broken up that earth, cleared it of woods and snakes. His people had grown in number; thanks to him, they were now acquainted with song, and the owners of the magic *Sampo*. Seated downcast before the fire on that June evening – because, even if the *Kalavela* does not say so, I am certain that it must have been an evening in June, every bit as white and dazzling as this one now – Väinämöinen realized that this last battle was to be one he could not win. Pain is not something that can be shared; each must pay his own dues. The great *runoilija* felt too old and weak to take on that last challenge along with all the rest; so he decided to go away, back to those still waters from which he had come, to the margins of the created world, the abode of Antero Vipunen and all the greatest shamans who, having left their bodies, wander around their empty carcasses as though around some ancient temple long since claimed by brambles.'

Here the pastor paused – for breath, I thought, or possibly for thought. But it seemed as if he were listening out for something, awaiting some sound. He went up to the window, straining his ears; I stayed where I was. But all that could be heard from outside was the sound of the wind in the trees. That seemed to bring him back to the present; he drained his glass of *koskenkorva* and carried on.

'Beware how you bring up your sons, you future generations – do not let them be lulled to sleep by strangers. Children who are cradled without gentleness, raised uncaringly, dragged up harshly, will not become intelligent, will never have the gift of wisdom, will never become men, even should they grow up strong and healthy and live for a hundred years! It was with these words, so many years earlier, that the old Väinämöinen had responded to the news of the death of Kullervo, son of Kalervo. On the evening of the great banquet, no one would have thought to speak of it, to remind him of it – Kullervo after all had killed the wife of Ilmarinen, the virgin of Pohjola, he had violated his own sister and finally taken his own life, throwing himself upon his sword. But thinking of the evil by which man is dogged – which worms its way even into those things which are most beautiful, which tracks them down wherever they are hidden –Väinämöinen bethought himself of the ferocious Kullervo and his wretched life. Such ferocity is more than a man's share. We find the seed of hatred on this earth and sow it along with the rye, believing it to be good. It was Untamo who sowed that hatred when he slaughtered the family of his brother Kalervo, burned down his village and dragged the only survivor, a pregnant woman, off to prison: the child who was born was Kullervo. His mother nurtured his hatred, fuelling his craving for revenge. He grew up in a state of slavery, and without memories, for there was nothing in his life to be remembered. From Untamo's kindred he received kicks instead of fondling, insults instead of gentleness, hatchets for splitting wood instead of toys. From his mother, he received a grounding in ruthlessness. Day after day she would look into his heart, uprooting any shoot of tenderness because she wanted his soul to be a desert. Kullervo never knew what childhood was.'

The room was sunk in glowing semi-darkness. Koskela lit a

candle, and his face appeared, etched out of the darkness by its light. His gestures cast a shadow on the wall, serving as background to his story. In those shadows I could see Untamo raising his knife, Kalervo's village going up in flames – scenes from another world, summoned up and sent dancing mysteriously upon the wall in front of me by Koskela's words, which put me in mind of some formula uttered during a spiritualist seance.

'When Untamo saw the bestiality that blinded that child's gaze, he was stricken with fear: he realized that that little creature would be the instrument of his own death. He ordered that he be put in a barrel and cast out to sea. But after three days and three nights the barrel was washed up on the shore, and Kullervo was found to be unscathed: the hatred burning within him had saved his life. Then Untamo ordered that a great pile of wood should be made, and that the child should be tied up in its midst; but when, after three days, the flames died down, Kullervo was still alive, up to his knees in ashes, and his eyes burned like the fire which was to have been his undoing. Then Untamo drove him from the village, hoping to exorcize the threat he posed. Kullervo was purchased by the smith Ilmarinen, who tried to make a good servant of him. But Kullervo was a beast, born to hate and destroy. He slaughtered the smith's wife, the beautiful virgin of Pohjola, and fled into the forests of the North, banished from the society of men for the atrocities he had committed. The old woman he met by the side of the black river separating the land of Kaleva from Tuonela, the kingdom of the dead, was certainly a demon. It was she who told him that his father, his mother and his sister were still alive, on the shore of the lake which bordered Lapland. "My hapless son, are you still wandering this world with your eyes open?" These were the words with which his mother greeted him. But not even family affection could deflect Kullervo from his brutish mission. In vain did his father attempt to teach him to make himself useful. He sent him off to fish; but Kullervo's hands were too powerful to simply hold the oars, they had been trained to crush, to wreck. He broke the rowlocks, shattered the keel. Then his father told him to pull on the nets and beat the water, so as to catch some fish. But Kullervo made mincemeat of the fish and reduced the oars to pulp.

In desperation, his father then told him to take a sledge and go off to pay the taxes.

'Perhaps your strength will serve you on the journey,' his father sighed. It was on Kullervo's return, as he was roaring through Pohjola's lands, knocking down trees and flattening the hillsides, that he met his sister and, failing to recognize her, raped her. When, returning home, he realized what he had done, Kullervo gave up all hope. "May I find death in the jaws of the howling wolf or the roaring bear, or in the belly of the barracuda!" he yelled amidst his tears, on his knees before his mother.

"No, my son, that will not help you, nor will time bring you solace or forgiveness until the whole of your allotted destiny has been played out," answered his mother, crushed by grief. For she knew that only when he had massacred the whole house of Untamo would her son be free of the hatred that she herself had planted in his heart. Now he had turned into a giant, twisted tree, one which no axe could dint.'

As he spoke, Koskela had become in turn a wolf, a bear, a barracuda. Now he was a tree, motionless in the middle of the room: his skin had become bark, his outstretched arms gnarled branches, waiting expectantly. He was breathing heavily: like the real trees outside, he rustled in the night wind.

'The day he left to wage war against Untamo, Kullervo did not know that he would never see his mother again, that with the conclusion of his mission his life too would end; that the pain which had driven him to it would be put out. His mother, like all mothers, sensed as much; but she could not hold him back. She had dreamed that he would have a happy life, that she would enjoy a calm old age beside him. Fate had decreed otherwise, and that fate was now being inexorably played out. In vain she begged her son to stay; she would rather have him alive and accursed than dead and liberated. But Kullervo was deaf to her entreaties, and proceeded to massacre all of Untamo's kith and kin, leaving their village a smoking wreck. When he returned home and found only the dog, Musti, he saw that this was the end. It was remorse that killed him; nothing else could have.'

Here Koskela broke off again, poured out another two glasses of *koskenkorva* and again downed his own in a single gulp. That night's story included many words I did not know, mention of many objects I had never heard of; but I didn't feel that I could interrupt him and ask for explanations. Even when I lost the thread, I was captivated just hearing him speak. In the darkness, I could no longer read his lips. His eyes were two craters in his lunar face, his mouth a black abyss, a volcano that spat out sounds; it was those I now followed, rather than the words. Above all, I liked the names: Antero, Kullervo, Untamo, Kalervo. They were not merely names, they were magic formulae. It was as though, by pronouncing them, their owners would emerge alive from the pastor's throat, like so many monsters which he had been harbouring deep in his entrails, and wander around the room, bemoaning their fate and dancing around as though possessed.

'The fight against the evil which drove Kullervo to commit his crimes goes on to this day. Väinämöinen was right: we can do nothing against it. Human life bursts into flames, then burns and dies out without a jot of all the pain we bear within us being consumed. Quite the reverse: this insatiable animal feeds upon every man who comes into this world, upon every life which is added to the lives already here. It grows and grows, devouring everything around it, like those loathsome fish which live in the muddy depths of lakes where no algae grow. All we can do is to deny it its nourishment. If the world's evil feeds upon our lives, only without them will it grow hungry, and so die. That is why the killing must go on, why every war is good; why every death takes us nearer our goal!'

Now there was anger in the pastor's eyes. His irate shadow lashed the room, and I felt I had to get up from where I was sitting to protect myself. I flattened myself against the wall, that same wall that Koskela used to stare at during his hallucinations. I sounded out its cracks and lumps, my hands behind my back. I had the impression that they were mysterious signs, key to some rite of passage, and that that wall was the doorway to another world. In the guttering light of the candle I saw the figure of Kullervo in the *Kalevala* that lay open on the table, the painting by Gallen-Kallela that Koskela had showed me on several occasions. His eyes raised to the skies, his face distorted in a furious grimace, his fist firmly clenched, his whole appearance made me shudder. The red light falling in through the window was now becoming slowly tinged with grey. The sun was sinking behind the forests and a dense layer of salt-laden cloud was settling over the sleepless city. The pastor was waving his fist in front of the square of transparent window, but it no longer cast any shadow.

'What is the message of the cross, if not death? Powerless in the face of evil, God has at least tried to show us the way out!'

That night I dreamed that waves of soldiers were emerging silently from the sea and falling upon the city; they had black lumps instead of eyes. All that was to be seen of their faces was their mouths, twisted with effort. They were running through the streets of the town centre at breakneck speed, their steps echoing on the cobbles like the roll of a broken drum, swarming all over the place like so many black insects. They came pouring into the Suurtori, climbed the steps up to the cathedral and went down the other side. They were running but not stopping, never firing, they had no weapons. They went through the city, making their way through the terrified crowd, then vanished into the woods, dived into the lakes, never to re-emerge. Then suddenly we realized that it was they who were frightened of us, it was they who were fleeing. Then we ran after them, hoping to grab hold of them, but there were too many of them, they slipped through our grasp like shadows, like clouds in the sky, like mice. Then they were no more to be seen, and all that could be heard was our shouts as we ran after them.

I woke up with the feeling that I had not slept at all. My head ached, and there was a bitter taste in my mouth; the walls of the room looked softer in the pink dawn light. Something told me that it was late. The bell had not rung. Suddenly I understood. Walking slowly into the church – I was no longer in a hurry – I found the nurses somewhat flustered, muttering irritated comments without moving from their seats. The door of the sacristy was wide open; the half-empty bottle of *koskenkorva* was still on the table, and the *Kalevala* open at the page with the picture of Kullervo.

In the days following Koskela's departure, I clung to my studies as though to a life jacket. When the time for my lesson came, I would shut myself in the sacristy and study every word I'd put down in my notebook, declining it in all possible cases, conjugating each verb in every voice I knew, down to the most tortuous forms of the passive, the conditional, even the past potential; undaunted now by irregular verbs with alternating consonants, I had in my head all the 'p's which became 'v's, the 'lke's which became 'lje's, the 'ht's which became 'hd's. Strong or weak, there was no stem of any verb I could not pick out in the forest of syllabic mutations, where it was enough to add one vowel to cause three consonants to disappear; then there were those nouns without so much as a diphthong, where the 'i's of the plural put paid to every syllable not protected by solid dentals. The only thing that sometimes floored me was polysyllabic stems, and then I would fill page after page getting them right, feeling an unhealthy pleasure at seeing those sheets so densely packed with words, those elixirs of grammar whose every line contained three or four rules, one entangled in the exceptions of another but always itself correct. When I had reached the end of my own notebook, when I'd exhausted my stock of headed notepaper from the Hotel Kämp, I had the nurses give me sheets of wrapping paper. I spread them out on the table as though they were maps of my personal campaigns, filling every last bit of them with formulae as unforgiving as equations, where every letter that

I wrote weighed heavy as lead in terms of sheer mental effort. Fragile as houses of cards but logically indestructible, those syntactical digests were my defence against an enemy who was attacking me from behind. I had no tanks, no bombardiers, and each day surprised me on a different front, drawing me into the open, far from reason's hiding-places, towards a chasm of gloomy, giddy thoughts. It was then that I needed all fifteen Finnish grammatical cases, the four forms of the infinitive, not to mention the negative pluperfect to keep my mind engaged, to drag it clear of that carpet bombing. Then I would even resort to declining my name, '*Sampo*', as a noun, one of those which have a slightly odd partitive plural, and *karjalainen* as an adjective – at least that was regular, as round and perfect as a circle. Once again, my name was all I had. The label coming unstitched from the neck of my jacket was my identity card, my sole claim to existence, the fragile line of communication allowing me to carry on restocking my trenches and resisting the temptation to disappear, to do away with myself, like the pastor, to go back into the darkness from which I had come. The words of Doctor Friari often came into my mind, when he had encouraged me to love the Finnish language, to abandon myself to it as one would to the arms of a loving woman. Then the fire that still burned beneath the ashes should have taken on new life: I'd been blowing on those embers for months, for months I had been coaxing into life a flame which would not take. The words came out of my mouth and disappeared like stones thrown into the sea; nothing of them stayed in my brain. My memory was nothing but a list of words, a dictionary, a conversation manual. Ilma – perhaps she was the answer; but I could not love Ilma without first knowing who I was. I could not offer her the heart of someone I did not know. Perhaps because I wished her well, I could not love her. Not even my feelings were really my own. I bore the name of the body I inhabited, but I did not have its heart. This was something that Doctor Friari had never understood, and I did not have the words to explain it to him. After all these months, I realized that I was as alone as I had been on that first day. The anguish which had nailed me to the bed that first afternoon was still within me, entire and unabated.

Had I been able to be at that man's side during his time in Finland, I am certain that today we would be able to laugh together about Sampo Karjalainen. We would have gone to Kappeli's, sat down in front of a tankard of beer and talked to each other about our experiences in the war, mine on board the Tübingen and his on the streets of Helsinki. Then even this grim winter would have seemed less dire, its snow and stars dispelling thoughts of darkness. I feel even more bitter reading these lines when I think how little it would have taken for him to have come through unscathed. If he had held on for another few weeks the war would have been over, Miss Koivisto would have been back in Helsinki and everything would have been different; because, however unfeeling, no human heart can hold out against a woman in love. A woman in love is a physical presence, a body which, of all those on earth, seeks out and desires only our own. We are animals, we are made of flesh and blood, we have need of the body in order to gain a sense of the soul. Of each lost love, it is the body that we mourn and, could we but keep it, even lifeless, even mute, but intact, we would make do with that. For bodies we are ready to build pyramids, and even after a hundred years a man is not dead until his body has been found. We refer to him as missing, we imagine him dragging out some kind of existence in a distant, hostile land, clinging grimly on to life, desperate to come home. We cannot help him, we cannot go out towards him, because anyone who has gone so far away is always in the wrong and must pay a price, a ransom. All we can do is wait for him, it is our duty to wait for him, and this may be a lifelong wait. Only the return of his body can free us from this waiting.

It is little consolation to me to see that my advice was valid: only a woman could have saved that man, and Miss Ilma almost succeeded. I had been right. My diagnosis had been correct; the medicine had been what was needed. But I had proffered it to the wrong patient.

These last pages are in a poor state. Some parts are stained with liquid, possibly koskenkorva, and the writing is smudged, though the basic meaning has not been lost. I found no trace of the second exercise book of which the author speaks, presumably used solely for studying the Finnish language, nor of the sheets of packing paper given him by the nurses. From this point onwards the document is no longer written in ink, but in indelible pencil. Although it is less methodical than the earlier parts, it shows a surer grasp of the language which this man had been so effortfully obliged to learn; even the mistakes are more academic, often due to the discrepancy between the spoken and the written language. All in all, it might indeed be said that that man had learned, or perhaps constructed, his own personal version of the Finnish language, a language all his own, handworked and roughly cut, where each word needed correcting, filing down, before it could come into complete possession of its meaning.

How such a language must have sounded is hard to imagine. Miss Koivisto says that he managed to make himself understood perfectly adequately, even if he had to reformulate his sentences several times before they became comprehensible. He would *alternate rudimentary and ungrammatical constructions with others taken from a printed book or idiomatic phrases, sometimes used in the wrong context. He had no concept of linguistic registers, and would use adjectives taken from the Bible alongside nouns he had heard in the bar at the Kämp. He did not give the impression of knowing the rules, but seemed to have learned the inflected forms of words according to their usage. He did the same thing with verbs, preferring the simpler constructions of the impersonal passive. As a neurologist I still marvel at this feat. My scientific knowledge fails to explain how that man could have built himself up a personality out of nothing, forged a language for himself by sheer willpower. Clearly, our minds are infinitely more powerful than we know. Shamans, saints and madmen gain mastery of this lethal weapon in different ways, and sometimes it kills them. They stray into this unknown dimension and, in their delirium, bring us back scraps of it which we find indecipherable.*

It was only after the battle of Kuuterselkä, when the first wounded began to arrive back in Helsinki, that we realized what was really going on in the Karelian Isthmus. They were brought back to the city by night, so that people wouldn't see them, in lorries driven by the medical corps. I heard them arriving, saw them going into the misty courtyard; then I started to get dressed. I stayed seated on my bed, waiting for the nurses to come and call me. In the bruised light, their bandages looked the same colour as the gravel in the courtyard. They emerged from beneath the tarpaulins like ghosts, and we shepherded them slowly into the building, helping those who were incapable of walking. We took them to the innermost wing of the hospital, the one which also housed the visitors' quarters. They were almost all very young, more perturbed by what they had escaped than by the wounds themselves. They were unwilling to speak of life at the front, and answered the nurses' questions in monosyllables. Many were running fevers, and for several days all that could be seen of them was their outline, standing out beneath the sheets. The others too stayed lying down, staring at the ceiling or, if they were able to get up, going into the courtyard, where they wandered around smoking cigarettes they never finished. The few veterans from the Winter War told us about the breakthrough at Valkeasaari; they said that they had never seen such aggression, that this time the Russians were really bringing out the big guns. The line of defence at Kuuterselkä, too, had been breached with the utmost ease. But how could anyone hold out against such force? Both the nurses' questions and the soldiers' answers suggested a shared concern, hitherto kept hidden, the nervous allusion to a place which no one dared to name. I had looked for the places I was hearing about on the map; without exception, they formed a ring around Viipuri, a circle which was closing in. People discussed the news in the papers without ever making explicit mention of the name of the great city, almost as though they thought it would bring bad luck, as though not naming it would cause the Russians to forget about its existence. In the hospital refectory the patients would gather around the soldiers returning from the Isthmus and listen carefully to what they had to say, seeking the slightest sign that the Russians were directing their attack elsewhere, that Viipuri was in the clear, and anything would serve to bear out that conviction: current rumours, letters from the front, the most abstruse strategic reflections from some returning soldier. People would reassure themselves by repeating that the capital of Karelia was too well-defended, that the Russians would never run the risk of incurring the huge losses that such an attack would incur. The

Germans were retreating, Leningrad was not in danger. Why would the Russians persist in attacking Viipuri?

In the middle of June, three of the remaining beds in the visitors' quarters were occupied, and I was no longer alone; but only for a few days, because my companions were three Russian officers who had been taken prisoner, and it was not long before they were transferred elsewhere. During their stay I listened to them curiously – their language was so different from Finnish. Pretending to study my notebook, I observed their gestures and their faces. So, that was what Russians were like. I thought of what Koskela had said, of the Uspenski Cathedral, of Ilma and her fear. The soldiers had occupied the three beds on the other side of the big room; the red-tiled floor ran between us like a frontier. They too were watching me in their turn; when they smoked, sometimes they would toss me the odd cigarette. I would nod my thanks, expressing my gratitude by lighting up immediately; then I would let them burn without actually smoking them, because they were so strong and bitter. One of the soldiers had been wounded in the foot, and moved around on crutches; the others too clearly had facial wounds, since their heads were bandaged. They stayed shut up in the room all day, with two guards watching over them from the corridor. When I came back, late at night, I would find them asleep, their uniforms neatly folded on their small iron trunks, their boots at the foot of their bed. I could see the tips of the guards' cigarettes glowing in the corridor, and this I found somehow reassuring: it was not that I was afraid of the Russians, but I liked to think that the guards were watching over me, too, warding off the oppressive dreams which thrust themselves upon me in the loneliness of sleep. The Russians' presence had livened up the visitors' quarters, made them somehow more welcoming. One night, after I had managed to lay hands on a bottle of spirits at the Kämp, I went back to the hospital earlier than usual, hoping to find the Russians still awake, as indeed they were, playing a game of cards. They invited me to sit with them; I understood nothing of the game, but I looked at the gilded figures on the cards, and they reminded me of the saints in the Uspenski Cathedral. The bottle was received with hearty slaps on the back, was passed round and very soon emptied; we consoled ourselves with cigarettes, of which there was no shortage, and also devised some form of conversation, using gestures and scraps of words which we spelled out in the air. One of the three, the one with the red stripe on his tunic, even spoke a sort of bastardized Finnish: he would throw one word out on top of another, then separate them with his hands. The verbs, however complicated, he would simply mime, as though he were quite used to expressing himself in that fashion. He showed me dog-eared photographs of women and children, the shape of whose eyebrows resembled his own, taking them out of his wallet and then replacing them with the greatest care. He also tried to explain to me which Russian city he came from, with the aid of an imaginary map of Russia, drawn with one finger on the wall. I went to my trunk to get the map of Europe which Koskela had used during our lessons, the one he'd used to describe the misguided migrations made by the Finno-Ugrians; but it didn't serve much purpose, since it stopped at the Urals. When we opened it out on the floor, the city this man came from turned out to be two tiles beyond the edge.

'*Suuri*, Russia on *suuri maa!*' he exclaimed, laughing and banging the floor with his fist. That night in June was the last time I felt the warmth of another human turned in my direction, the last time I spoke heart to heart with one of my fellow men. The next morning, when I came back from mass, I found the three beds empty, the mattresses rolled up. It seemed to me that I could still see the outline of Russia which the officer had sketched out with his finger on the wall.

Now it was a pastor from the nearby cathedral who came to say mass in the hospital chapel. But after having heard Koskela's sermons, those of the new officiant struck me as glib and infantile; his use of language was unsubtle, his words came straight from the Mass Book, I could understand them without any difficulty, and hence heard them without interest. I offered the newcomer my help as a sacristan, but I did not seek his friendship, indeed I made sure that I kept my distance. I talked with him enough to ensure that church business went smoothly, but no more than that. Yet, despite my unresponsiveness, the new pastor showed me considerable kindness: noticing my interest in language, perhaps on the nurses' suggestion, he gave me a new notebook, with plain white pages. But my attitude towards him remained unchanged. As I had done with Koskela, in the morning I would wash the floors and dust the holy objects, in the evening I would light the candle before the service and put away the missals at the end. But the intimacy I had established with Koskela was not something that could ever be repeated; it was the fruit of long and careful nurturing, and I had no desire to dull its memory by finding a substitute. The new pastor did not use the sacristy; he prepared his sermons elsewhere, and came into the little room just to hang up his hat. I had put Koskela's *Kalevala* and the bottle of *koskenkorva* back into the little cupboard and sometimes, in the evening after the service, when the pastor had left, I would stay on there for a time, thinking about the past. In my hands, the bottle did not replenish itself; when I had finished it, it remained resolutely empty. But even that empty bottle served as a reminder of my old friend. I took it away, together with the *Kalevala*, and put it in my little trunk, as though it were a relic. The faded label and the lingering sweetish smell reminded me of my first afternoons in the sacristy, with the crackling stove and the ice on the window panes: they spoke to me of a world which now seemed infinitely far away.

One sultry evening, when I was tossing and turning in my bed, unable to sleep, a nurse came in and asked me to run to get the pastor, saying it was urgent. The condition of one of the wounded who had arrived the previous day had suddenly worsened; he was a private, a member of an anti-tank division, one of whose legs had been amputated. I remembered him, because he was the only member of the convoy whom we had taken off the lorry on a stretcher. Wounded at the battle of Kuuterselkä, he had been left untended for several hours, since he had been thrown into a crater made by a mine, under Russian fire. The stretcher-bearers had not been able to reach him until the evening, when they had taken him into no-man's-land. He had caught diphtheria some days earlier, and had to be transferred immediately so as to avoid infecting his fellow troops, and that was how he had arrived in Helsinki. Extremely weak from loss of blood, that night he had also had a bad attack of dysentery and was completely dehydrated; the doctor did not give him many hours to live. I leapt out of bed and ran out into the courtyard, then down Unioninkatu, where my footsteps rang out on the stone still warm from the day's strong sun. I could feel a throbbing in my temples, and sweat was running down my back. In no time I was at the Suurtori, then I was passed the cathedral and found myself knocking at the door of the low block of flats on the eastern side of the square. In words mangled by my heavy breathing, I explained the situation to the pastor, who followed me anxiously into the street, panting and buttoning up his clothes. The wounded man had been taken into a room the size of my own, situated next to the casualty department, away from the other wards, and used for infectious patients. He was the room's sole occupant, lying in the furthest away of the six beds, and a nurse was wiping his forehead with cold cloths which she was picking out of a bucket at her feet. At the other side of the bed, the doctor, in his shirt sleeves, was taking his pulse. The room smelled of human flesh, of blood and faeces, laced with a dash of carbolic acid, against which the faint breeze coming in through the open window battled in vain. An oil lamp, attached to the bars of the bed, cast an oblique light over the sick man, and it bounced off the metal of the other beds, projecting a pattern of flickering, intersecting lines on to the ceiling.

'Is he conscious?' the pastor asked under his breath; the doctor nodded, and drew back. The nurse too picked up her bucket and went to stand at the foot of the bed. When the pastor entered the strip of bluish light cast by the lamp, his features hardened, made suddenly prominent by deep, cold shadows, his eyes like two empty pits. As he leant over the sick man, the crucifix around his neck swung suddenly from side to side, and his shadow seemed to grow larger on the wall.

'Father! My leg hurts – it's all hot, and wet!' the soldier moaned. Standing beside the bed, the pastor had opened his breviary; holding it towards the bluish light, he began to say a prayer.

'You can't get through there, father! Don't go that way! It's dangerous!' the solider was saying, suddenly seizing hold of the pastor's jacket. The nurse came up from the other side of the bed and moistened his forehead, whispering words which seemed to comfort him.

'That's the road to Mustamäki, that white line down there. On the other side of it are the Russians. That's where they're firing from! They've taken possession of the railway, they're advancing with their tanks!'

The wounded man continued to thrash around, and his blurred speech drowned out the pastor's voice. He was looking at the breviary open above him as though it were a scalpel poised for yet further action.

'Don't go that way, father! They're not afraid of dying, they're not like us. That's what you said, father! They go to Heaven, but we don't!'

The nurse had removed her cloth and was still trying to calm him, but now with no success; as though possessed by some new strength, the dying man was now lifting himself up on to his elbows.

'Father Koskela! Don't leave me alone! I don't want to die!' the soldier shouted, and his cry hung on in the silence.

The pastor's prayer rang out, clear as a bell, falling upon the death-laden air like disinfectant. He performed the last rites with sharp, clear-cut gestures. Then he remained kneeling by the dead man for a few minutes, murmuring a psalm before moving off, together with the doctor. I heard their steps dying away at the end of the corridor. The nurse had gone off to fetch water to wash the corpse, and I stayed on beside him alone; leaning against the wall, I looked at his sweat-veiled face with some alarm, stared at his twisted mouth and stiffened fingers, just visible above the sheet. That man had seen Koskela; a few moments before he went off to die. My friend Olof Koskela. Perhaps he was still out there somewhere. I looked towards the window through eyes made dim with tears; a few wan stars were floating in the pallid sky. I imagined the pastor lying on his back on the ground, his eyes wide open, looking at those same stars that I could see, fading beyond the window.

In the registers of the Finnish Lutheran Church which I consulted in the offices of the Tuomiokirkko, the Pastor Olof Koskela was said to have fallen in the battle of Kuuterselkä on 14 June 1944. It was not known where he was buried. A short note attached to the file gave a resume of the military report describing the circumstances of his death and the finding of his body, by the road which runs between the turn-off for Kuuterselkä and the village of Mustamäki. The Finnish troops' hasty retreat from the Karelian Isthmus probably meant that the bodies of the fallen could not be transported behind the lines.

What follows is the last letter sent by Ilma Koivisto, which the author at some point copied into his document. In fact, Miss Koisvisto told me that she had also written a fourth letter, which she had never sent, and which still has in her possession; she said that I could read it if I felt it might help me in my reconstruction of events. I did not think it appropriate to probe any further into the private world of a woman who had already suffered so much. I would prefer that the last words addressed by Ilma Koivisto to the man she believed to be Sampo Karjalainen continue to be known only to the person who wrote them.

Viipuri, 19 June 1944

Dear Sampo,

I don't know what sense it makes to carry on writing to you, but I can't resist throwing these few words into your silence.

To be honest, they are words which it is better not to carry around inside oneself, because after a time they will begin to rot, infecting everything around them like gangrene. Each day I've waited for a letter, each morning when the post was being distributed I thought I'd hear my name. I even thought that something might have happened to you, that you had gone away, had disappeared, had died. But, in that case, my letters would have been returned. So I know that you've read them, and this knowledge I find even more hurtful. But there seems to me to be something false, something fabricated about your unresponsiveness; it is a bit like the personal war you are waging against the figments of your memory. Here, war – I mean real war – has arrived in earnest; the front is a few kilometres away, we can see the German planes bombing the Russian lines. Viipuri itself is threatened; the twentieth regiment is lining up against the imminent attack. Tomorrow we are going to a field hospital beyond the river Vuoksi, where all the wounded from this sector of the front will be brought. We are needed everywhere: everywhere there are soldiers with shattered limbs who do not yet know whether they will live or die. I have never seen so many dead all in one place, so much life draining out of bodies so fast. It is a tragic irony that with so many memories being abandoned by their legitimate owners, you cannot find one which meets with your approval, and persist in wanting one all of your own. We are leaving the refugee centre with a great sense of foreboding; months of work will be destroyed by bombing, or fall into the Russians' hands; but then in war everything is made to be destroyed, perhaps including our own friendship. That's why it was doomed from the start. But it's my fault, I was asking for too much. I instantly demanded from you that touch of the infinite which human relationships can never provide. Both for better and for worse, we can never perceive the infinite; even when we believe that we are the bearers of immense suffering, in reality we are like ants carrying crumbs. God measures out the pain that each of us can bear, the least and the most. Everything is bearable, until we die of it. Nothing of us outlasts us, and if some pain outlives us for some time, it is only in order to be sure that it has killed us well and truly. People have been evacuated out of Viipuri for some time, ever since the rout at Kuuterselkä. The Russians broke through our defences all along the front. Yesterday refugees arrived from as far away as Petroskoi, a whole lorryload, stuffed to the gunwales with people and furniture, hoping to be taken in by relatives. But there's no one left here now: the city's empty, its only occupants are stray dogs and horses driven mad by fear. Dear Sampo, this is the last letter I'll be writing you. By the end of the page, each of us will be free to suffer again on our own, free to reclaim our solitude. All in all, this is the condition to which man is best suited; it is the ideal condition for whole-heartedly pursuing our own self-preservation, the only real task God has assigned to us. If one day I come back to Helsinki, I shall not look for you; I shall not want to remember you, and this time I shall not even feel sorry for you. I shall go and remove you from the tree of happy memories. I didn't tell you, but my tree is also capable of forgetting. I'll go and find it on my own, one evening towards the end of winter like the time when I took you there, and your memory will melt away like snow in the breath of the sea wind. Forgetting is the only form of defence left to us; nothing which has been forgotten has the power to harm us any more; yet there you are, mercilessly scrutinising your consciousness in the hopes of digging up a few shreds of memory. I shall forget, I shall recover from this illusion as I have from others, but you won't: all this is something that you will want to remember. And I know that you will keep my letters, that you will reread them. Not for what they contain, but because they too will have turned into precious relics of your reconstituted past. But be warned: for many years to come, these words – which you today have wanted to ignore – will continue to haunt you. And then you will be defenceless in the face of regret; all the time that you have so greedily hoarded, unpicking the embroidery of the days life offered you, will become snarled up in hopeless disarray; because it is not yours, it is the fruit of plunder. Time is not sewn patiently from little, ordinary things, it is not a carpet of words and silences, of glances and moments within which memory slowly envelops us.

It's a lovely summer's evening. The sun is sinking into the sea, lighting up the trunks of the trees, catching the buds of new resin on their bark, making the streamlets glitter. There was a time when this landscape would have gladdened my heart; I would have run down to the bright shore, to the waves of our own sea, unthreatening as a lake. But today this brightness holds no joy for me, and the long shadows on the meadows put me in mind of crosses. Death is all around me, and something within me, too, is dying: the affection that I felt for you, the faith I had in you. Now that their place is empty, I see how big it was. Like a bomb crater, it will fill up with water and with mud; but time will make the grass grow even there and, before long, the coots will nest there too. You, Sampo, are a plunderer of time, but I allow time to grow, and thrive.

Goodbye,
Ilma

Ilma's last letter arrived yesterday, together with the news of the fall of Viiipuri. This one too I read under the tree of happy memories, and now it's with the others in my jacket pocket. Once again, I did not understand it all, though I could not fail to see that it contained harsh words. It had clearly been written in a hurry, and I had difficulty copying it out. The steady, rounded hand to which I was accustomed had given way to one that was flatter, less legible. The margins were no longer neatly aligned, with the syllables conveniently marked off; now the words were twisted and choked, as though the writer had not had the time or indeed the inclination to make them comprehensible, and there were crossings out and blank spaces. Even the letters of my name on the envelope might have been written by a different hand; reading them was like hearing myself summoned by an unknown person. But nothing matters any more after what happened today at Katajanokka.

The End Foretold

Ilma was right in saying that everything is bearable until it kills us. Man's struggle against pain is a war where each of the two sides has its own rightful role. The winner acknowledges the dignity of the defeated, even when it is a death sentence. But my war was of another kind; it was a war in which I was my own enemy. And now I have lost it. To spare myself would have made no sense; there are no prisoners in this kind of challenge.

For days now, the city has been sweltering under a sultry cloak of haze. The air is heavy, dust-laden, full of animal smells; the sea gives out a bitter smell of rotten seaweed. As they cross the bay to reach the market, the fishing boats create waves which linger on behind them, slow to close up. Night and day follow one another under the same uncaring, leaden sky, whiter where the sun is; even at night it carries on glowing, like embers buried under ash. Beneath this stagnant air, the city barely moves; it trembles slightly as the trams pass, like the faded scenery of some old theatre. Houses and blocks of flats seem on the point of crumbling away, as though some imperceptible underground explosion had silently snapped the iron framework of their reinforcements.

Last night a land wind brought cool air, and this morning clouds streaked with violet massed above the city, shutting out the horizon from all sides. After my stint in the laundry, I had gone down to the port to enjoy the freshness, and walked as far as the point at Katajanokka. There was a lot of coming and going in the harbour at Pohjoissatama. A train was worming its way along the shore, where a big old rusty merchantman was moored. Beside me, a group of sailors seated on the ballast were watching the ships as they passed in front of the wharf, and the plumes of smoke from vessels further out to sea. A gunboat was coming out of the port, probably on its way to the Isthmus; it was heading in our direction, cleaving the water powerfully as it went, sending up wings of foam. Black in the black water, all flags flying, it was a daunting sight; we could see the sailors running busily to and fro on the deck. Now it was passing right in front of us, an imposing hulk of riveted sheet metal, bristling with cannon, teeming with shouting sailors. Two whistles from its siren threw the whole bay into a state of alert. One of the sailors on the ballast pointed to it, saying:

'That's German goods! It arrived here from Danzig in 1943, Walhalla, it's called. We repainted it ourselves in the shipyards at Suomenlinna!'

I too watched the ship as it sailed by, the blue cross snapping in the wind to the stern, smoke pouring from the smoke stack, adding further grey to the dull sky. Behind the city darker clouds were now rising, swollen with rain. The sailors who'd been sitting beside me on the ballast were now walking away, caps in their hands, down along the side of the hill. Even when they had disappeared from sight, I could still hear snatches of what they were saying, as though from another world. Now I was quite alone on Katajanokka Point, and fate was preparing its show for me alone.

I was gripped by a sudden, almost physical sense of unease; it was as though my mind had not yet received the message which my eyes had sent it. My face to the wind, I carried on looking at the ship, more because it happened to be before my eyes than out of any genuine curiosity. It was then, and only then, that I saw the large white rust-streaked letters on its towering hull: 'Sampo Karjalainen'. I have no words to describe the sensation that came over me: rather than surprise, or disbelief, my predominant feeling was one of fear: at first it felt like a blow, a sudden lash to the defenceless brain, then, like a poison, it slowly seeped into every vein in my body. I let out a cry; but even a thousand cries would not have been enough. A cruel God has fashioned us in such a way that pain never bursts out all at one time, tearing us limb from limb; filters in mind and body intervene to slow the process down, to make us fully present at our suffering, so that we may sound out each portion of ourselves as it goes into agony, gasping and wheezing and powerless to die. That was what I experienced that morning on Katajanokka Point, nailed to the spot by that sight, my mind darkened by a maelstrom of thought. So that was it: that name, which I had always believed to be my own, written on the discoloured label of my seaman's jacket, was nothing other than the name of a warship. Thinking back to what the sailor had said, I realised why no one had ever linked my name with that of the warship 'Sampo Karjalainen'; it had not long been part of the Finnish navy. So no one had heard of it, and there was no knowing where it had previously been operating. So, did my jacket belong to one of the sailors on the warship? Indeed, was I one of them? And how had I landed up in Trieste? Or had I got hold of that jacket in some other way? So, who was I? What about the monogram on the handkerchief? What did those letters mean? They could not refer to the name of the ship. Whose initials were they? That volley of unanswerable questions toppled my certainties like bowling pins. The identity I had built up for myself with so much difficulty crumbled away in an instant, was blown sky-high by that explosion of white letters rising from the sea like a shout, an insult, a jeer. The warship 'Sampo Karjalainen' slipped slowly out towards the open sea, taking my name with it. Trieste, the Tübingen, Doctor Friari, Stettin, the Ostrobothnia, Ilma, Koskela, they were all whirling around in the kaleidoscope of my mind, turning every image into so many unfamiliar fragments. I was not Sampo Karjalainen, perhaps I was not even Finnish; now, I was no one at all.

Paradoxically, this discovery – which in fact was taking me nearer to the truth – had the effect of utterly weakening my resolve. I no longer had the strength to search, to try to stay afloat. I was seized by an irresistible urge to let myself founder, to disappear into the innermost recesses of my twisted mind. It no longer made sense to carry on seeking my real name, my real past. Eventually, I had indeed become Sampo Karjalainen, but not the one I dreamed of, with a house, a past, a family awaiting him. I was a non-existent man, invented by a label on a seaman's jacket, a huge misunderstanding which had taken on life through a cruel coincidence of accidents of which I was unaware. No shadow of uncertainty any longer lay between me and a tragic fate which I could not avoid. Such knowledge as I had, believing that I could legitimately claim it as my own, might after all have nothing to do with my true story, with my true name. Just a short time ago, I had believed that my real past was at my fingertips as I walked the streets of Helsinki, had dreamed that I would sooner or later take complete possession of it; now it was disappearing before my very eyes, sucked away by that whirlpool of unquestionable truth. Because now I knew it: that was the truth.

Now I started running: away from the sea, into the densest tangle of streets, where I wandered like a madman. It seemed to me that the whole city was reading that name as it was paraded around the bay on the ship's hull, that the journalists from the Kämp, the nurses in the hospital, even the sick and wounded, had gone down to the shore to take a good look at it, and that they were now marching threateningly towards me, demanding an explanation. Now the black crowd was driving me back into that same sea by which I had arrived that distant winter morning: they were fending me off, they were rejecting me. They were punishing me for having deceived them. I could not make out their faces, all I saw was the odd profile, part of a face, a snarling mouth, an outstretched leg, a raised arm. Some were shrieking, others were responding with a raised fist. A hand would seize me, trying to knock me to the ground, another would grab me by the collar, shouting: 'Who are you?' I wandered around the city, no longer recognizing it, no longer distinguishing what I was imagining from what I saw. I jumped with fright at every approaching passer-by, I peered about me, frightened that I was going to be attacked. I drifted around in a daze, taking streets I'd never seen before. The blood beat in my temples, my eyes throbbed, my hands trembled. Anguish was slowly taking over, paralysing my every action, choking down my every thought. It began to rain, a monotonous downpour, without thunder or lightning, which drowned out all other sounds. The city could breathe at last; I too heaved a sigh of relief. The clouds above me seethed and swelled, seemed to be ever growing. A quiet earthquake was shaking skies where, during those long days of heat, a bewitched city had grown up, an evil mirror of the real one, made up of fog and clouds. I walked the streets dreaming that the warship too was part of that diabolical double game, that the rain would carry it away as well, and that the white letters of its name would dissolve like a mirage over the distant sea.

The cold water on my skin, my eyes, my face, lessened my terror somewhat; I felt its coldness running down my every limb, soothing and washing my wounds. I recognized the Bulevardi, went as far as the Esplanadi, then reached the hospital, still in the pouring rain.

I have been here all day, seated on my bed in the visitors' quarters, finishing writing these last pages. I have not been to mass, nor to the refectory; I have neither eaten nor drunk. It is late now; another night without darkness has fallen over the city. Now my mind is made up: I shall leave for the front at dawn with the first troop train. Over all these months I have believed that I was someone I am not. I have looked among these people for my race, my kith and kin; I have learned the language in which I thought I had once called my mother, but whose sounds in fact had maybe never issued from my mouth. I shall never know in which language my mother sang me her lullabies. My language – my real language – is lost for ever. It slipped away, together with my memory; seeped away into the sea, together with my blood, that night on the wharf in Trieste. Perhaps my memories are drifting around in the oceans like unnoticed oil slicks, perhaps the waves are carrying them to some distant beach where they will be scattered, or sink into the sand like foam. If I had not gone down into the port that morning, perhaps I would never have known the truth; or perhaps that moment would simply have been delayed, who knows by how long. I might have lived for another fifty years without ever coming across the 'Sampo Karjalainen'. One day, in some distant future, when I was old and tired, I might perhaps have been able to accept the truth as a joke played on me by destiny. A whole life lived inside a wrong name makes it the right one, turns falsehood into truth. Two steps away from death, I would have laughed in the face of anyone who had come to tell me that I was not Sampo Karjalainen. More probably, though, the relentless burden of unease which I had borne ever since my awakening on board the Tübingen would have grown heavier over time, would have crushed all my efforts to find myself a life. No country would have felt like home. Even when I was at my most convinced that I would indeed be able to rediscover my past, I often had the feeling that I was moving in the wrong direction. Such faint traces of myself as I did occasionally come upon in my ravaged mind led elsewhere; and yet, as soon I began to follow them, they became indistinct. Perhaps I should never have taken up Doctor Friari's suggestion, never have thwarted the fate which had taken me to Trieste. That was my path, and I have strayed from it. I had the gall to make a choice; but in this world we have no choices. Or perhaps my destiny was precisely this: to come all this way, to learn Finnish, to become a Finn, even if I have never really become one. All in all, by now I owe this country everything; or rather, I owe it such little as I have managed to become. Without even knowing who I was, without asking for anything in exchange, it lent me a name, a language. In its hour of need, it took me in; all it required to be accepted, to be recognized as one of its own, was a name tape sewn into a sailor's jacket. A letter from an unknown doctor in the German army was enough to ensure me a bed and a succession of hot meals. So, because I am called Sampo Karjalainen, and because I speak Finnish, I shall go and fight for this country at dawn, and if I have not succeeded in being a real Finn in life, at least I shall be one in death. On the cross which they will place upon my grave, the name I bear will at last be mine. Mine alone; completely mine. I am leaving you my story, reader, so that you will make a memory of it. In this way I, who will live on in no one's memory, who, when alive, never existed, will be able to die hoping to be remembered.

Here Sampo Karjalainen's manuscript comes to an end. The notebook itself has several more pages, with various telephone numbers, addresses and the names of some places in Southern Karelia. Folded into the notebook I also found a plan of the City of Helsinki, torn out from a telephone directory, and a few tram tickets. Between the last page and the cover is a pressed leaf, probably from a service tree, which has left a green mark on the paper. Ilma Koivisto claims that it is a leaf from the tree of happy memories. The cover bears the initials S.K., in Indian ink, similar to those embroidered on the handkerchief which was found together with the manuscript. War Office file n. 37895 tells us that private Sampo Karjalainen, who enlisted as a volunteer on 24 June 1944 and was assigned to the third division of the frontier guards, fell in the battle of Ihantala, but there is no mention of where he is buried. Perhaps he lies not far from his only friend, the Pastor Olof Koskela, in some mass grave beside the road to Mustamäki. Perhaps he was crushed beneath the tracks of a tank, and nothing of his body now remains. No one knows how the author of this manuscript met his death – this man whom I decided should be called Sampo Karjalainen. I, today, know who Sampo Karjalainen really was; that is why I have come to Helsinki to look for him: to make up for my wretched mistake, to give him back, if not his memory, at least his true identity and a place to which he can return. But the war carried me far away from him, prevented me from reaching him in time. Only today have I been able to accomplish my mission, and now it is too late.

Epilogue

While we were still anchored off Trieste, a few days after the departure of the convoy which took Sampo Karjalainen towards his death, Doctor Friedrich Reiner came in person to call on me on board the Tübingen. It was the evening before we set sail for North Africa. The sailors were making the final adjustments by the light of the ship's lanterns. A strong bora was blowing, hurling itself upon the ship with all its force; the autumn sky was filling up with clouds, glowing pink in the light of the setting sun. I was lying low in my study when the watch officer informed me of the doctor's arrival. The gust of wind that entered the room with him was as chilling as the news that he brought with him. He placed a package on the table – it was tied up with shoe laces, and wrapped up in a blue-striped pocket handkerchief with the initials S.K. embroidered on the edge – then proceeded to undo it with a solemn air. It contained a military identification tag engraved with the name Stefan Klein and the number 97840028, an empty wallet, an Italian railway ticket and a piece of crumpled paper, folded into four. On inspection, this turned out to be a document issued by the Italian navy, granting a fortnight's special leave, starting from 7 September 1943, to the soldier Massimiliano Brodar, born in Trieste on 6 December 1916 and resident in Via San Nicolo 10. Noting my bewildered expression, Doctor Reiner unbuttoned his greatcoat and began to explain.

Stefan Klein had been an agent working for the military secret service. Until August 1943 he had been in Finland, working as a military instructor for the Finnish navy. After the Italian armistice he had been promptly transferred to the zone of operations on the Adriatic coast, at Trieste, with the task of infiltrating the Italian forces and providing information aimed at averting possible hostile operations on the part of the former allies. The son of an Italian mother, Agent Klein spoke Italian fluently. This was what Doctor Reiner had learned from district headquarters. He had immediately sent a telegram to Klagenfurt; shortly afterwards, that same morning, a patrol from the security battalion, reconnoitring a sector of the Carso in search of partisans, had come upon the body of Stefan Klein, killed together with other soldiers taking orders from Salo. He was wearing the uniform of an Italian infantryman; several objects had been found about his person, though only the tag had enabled him to be identified. At first, Doctor Reiner could not remember where he had seen a similar handkerchief, but those initials were somehow vaguely familiar. The information provided by district headquarters came like a bolt from the blue. In all likelihood Agent Klein, who had come straight to Trieste from Helsinki, had attacked the soldier called Brodar at the railway station in order to lay hands on an Italian uniform and thus infiltrate the enemy forces more easily, dressing his victim in his own clothes so as to avoid suspicion, but forgetting completely to empty the pockets of his sailor's jacket ... Some days later, however, Stefan Klein had been tracked down by the partisans, and shot. Massimiliano Brodar's leave permit, which had been in the lining of his jacket, had probably been overlooked during the search. The man found in such desperate straits on the quayside near Trieste Railway Station, the man whom I had cared for and helped regain the use of language, was therefore Massimiliano Brodar. It was not his name which appeared on the label inside the jacket he was wearing, but that of the Finnish warship 'Sampo Karjalainen', the former German 'Walhalla', on which Agent Klein had served as an instructor before being sent on assignment to the zone of operations on the Adriatic coast.

This is the true story of the author of the manuscript, of the man whom I had caused to call himself Sampo Karjalainen. That was what I had come to tell him, if only I had found him still alive.

In the long months spent on board the Tübingen, just waiting for that awful war to finish, I often thought about that man, and tried to explain to myself how I could have come to make such a mistake. It was undoubtedly my blind attachment to my country which led me to take him for a Finn; and it was an equally blind self-confidence which led me to believe that that label was the proof of his identity. Instinctively, I did my utmost to save that unknown Finnish man whom war had cast my way. But, in reality, it was my own salvation I was seeking. As I had done in Hamburg, by helping a compatriot, I believed once again that I was atoning for my father's crime. This had been a lifelong obsession with me. For me, the death of my father – who had been murdered, having been unjustly accused of Communist subversion – became a crime that must be expiated. I took his place at the court martial which sentenced him to death, and for all these years I have been trying relentlessly to right a wrong which was not my own. Today I realise that this has been my whole life's work, that I have spent my days making amends for him, seeking a pardon that neither he nor or I were called upon to ask for. Every sailor who came to seek medical assistance in the Finnish church in Hamburg was my father's executioner, shaking with fever, seeking help. On each occasion, I could kill him or save him. And I saved him, time *after time, and his thanks were my absolution. But that was not enough: the whole of Finland had to absolve me, every single Finn had to pass through my hands in order that the pardon be complete. Had I found Massimiliano Brodar alive, I might have managed to shake off this past. Giving him back his name, his life – that would have set me free. But as it is, I carry on with my work of expiation, moving from one crime to another, because even after all this time I still feel myself a Finn, and as a child a priest like Koskela taught me that life is a matter of repentance, of punishing ourselves for ever being born. This unforgiving fatherland killed my own father; it drove me into exile, offered me nothing but affliction, and I yearn for it and curse it to this day. We come into this world in one place only, and only there do we belong. Sooner or later, the globetrotter who leaps from one identity to another like an acrobat on a trapeze will lose his footing, find himself down on the ground, pinned down, well-travelled though he be, by the memory of a few houses and a dusty road. When the hour of death draws near, even those who have spent their whole lives claiming they do not have a country will hear the sudden call of the place where everything began, and where they know they are awaited. There, and there only, everything will always be the same, each smell, each colour, each sound in its right place. When we go home, memory vanishes; and, with it, pain. When end and beginning meet, it means nothing has happened. All was a dream within another dream, and perhaps man too is the stuff of dreams.*

It has now been snowing for some hours, but the sky is none the lighter for it; it remains as louring and furrowed as the roof of a cave. The daylight has drained away like the remains of a doused fire, and remnants of smoky light linger in the streets. Now there is nothing to keep me in Helsinki. This evening I shall take the boat for Stockholm, then on to Hamburg. Before leaving, I asked Miss Koivisto to go with me to the visitors' quarters where Sampo Karjalainen lived. I wanted to stay there just for a few moments, to think things over.

So here I am, sitting on his bed, bed number six, looking out at the snow falling gently over the courtyard. It's all very quiet; lamplight, reflected on the snow, is sending a faint shadow of window bars on to the wall. A bell is ringing, probably calling people to mass. I get up and go into the courtyard, then follow indistinct figures making their way towards the little wooden church, their footsteps creaking in the snow. Inside, there is a good smell of wax and burning wood. Two candles are burning on the altar. A soldier is arranging the missals on the benches, hanging the gilded letters of the day's psalms up on the wall, opening the breviary on the lectern. I stare at him in the faint light, trying to catch a glimpse of his face in the flickering candlelight. I would like to go closer, I would like to talk to him. Then I decide against it, retrace my steps back into the middle of the courtyard and stay there in the darkness, watching the falling snow.